DOG TRAINING
IN NO TIME

DOG TRAINING IN NO TIME

How to Understand and Train Your Dog in Just Minutes a Day

CAROLINE DAVIS and KEITH DAVIS

Reader's Digest

The Reader's Digest Association, Inc.
Pleasantville, New York/Montreal

A READER'S DIGEST BOOK

This edition published by The Reader's Digest Association by arrangement with Hamlyn,
a division of Octopus Publishing Group Ltd,
2–4 Heron Quays, London E14 4JP

Photographer: Angus Murray

FOR READER'S DIGEST
U.S. Project Editor: Jane Sherman
Canadian Project Editor: Pamela Johnson
Project Designer: George McKeon
Executive Editor, Trade Publishing: Dolores York
Creative Director: Michele Laseau
Director, Trade Publishing: Christopher T. Reggio
Vice President and Publisher, Trade Publishing:
  Harold Clarke

Library of Congress Cataloging-in-Publication Data

Davis, Caroline, 1961-
   Dog training in no time : how to understand and train your
dog in just minutes a day / Caroline Davis, Keith Davis.
      p. cm.
   Includes bibliographical references (p.) and index.
   ISBN 0-7621-0440-6
   1. Dogs--Training. 2. Dogs--Behavior. 3. Human-
animal communication. I. Davis, Keith, 1956- IL Title

SF431.D37 2004
636.7'0887--dc21
                                    2003054816

For Reader's Digest products and information,
visit our website:
   www.rd.com (in the United States)
   www.readersdigest.ca (in Canada)

Printed in China

1 3 5 7 9 10 8 6 4 2

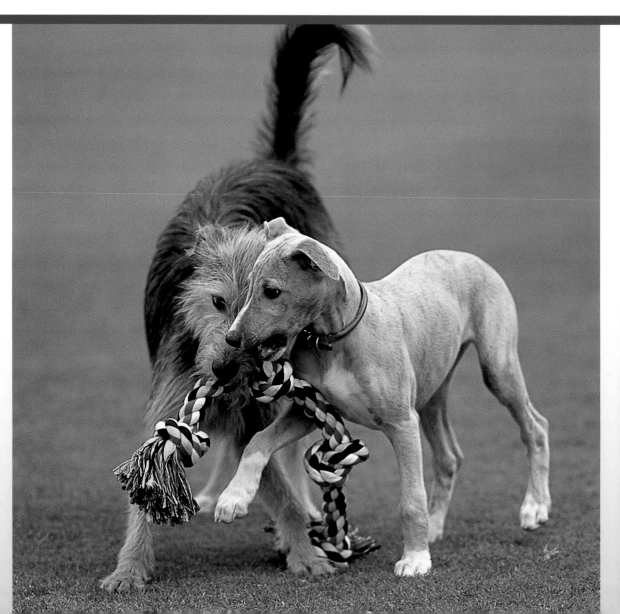

contents

INTRODUCTION

A dog is the ultimate companion. He won't judge your sins (real or imagined), get angry with you, lie to you, or cheat you. He may become miserable if you treat him badly, but he will never blame you. A dog's innocence and trust in you are complete.

It's well known that dogs are great stress relievers. They will happily listen to your daily moans and groans, celebrate with you when no one else is there to share special moments, and comfort you in your hour of need.

Many people, young and old alike, regard their dog as part of the family.

However, things aren't quite so rosy if you have a dog who nearly knocks you over when he greets you, won't let you sit on your favorite chair, soils in the house, is aggressive toward people and other animals, chews anything he can get his teeth on, and ignores the commands you give. That's when having a dog is simply anything but fun!

Handling and training your dog correctly from puppyhood helps keep problems from developing, and retraining an adult dog can often correct those that already exist. The knack is in knowing just how to go about it, and this book will give you training methods that are easy to understand and implement. You don't need expensive equipment or a degree in dog psychology—just some common sense, a willingness to learn how your dog's mind works, and the desire to turn him into a wonderful companion that everyone will love.

How to use this book

While we should not attribute our human characteristics to dogs, they are intelligent enough to perform many actions that their owners require of them, provided these actions are requested in a way that dogs find rewarding.

With this principle in mind, owners have to be clever, too, and find a way of training their dogs that works quickly and effectively. This book explains how to achieve this ideal; more precisely, it shows you how to speak "dog" so that you can communicate well with your four-legged friend.

Trying to do everything at once rarely works effectively. If you use the advice given here as a series of stepping stones, you'll find that the level of training for which you are aiming comes more easily to both you and your dog. However, some areas of obedience training complement others.

HE OR SHE?

Throughout this book, we have referred to dogs as "he," but unless otherwise stated, the advice given is equally applicable to female dogs.

For example, once you have taught your dog to sit, lying down and rolling over should come easily to him.

There are no set time limits for how long it should take to fully train a dog—in fact, setting time limits can be counterproductive if the owner thinks his dog is not progressing as he should. The length of time it takes to achieve success very much depends on the individual aptitude of both owner and dog.

Changing established behavior such as aggression, barking, chasing other animals, and car travel problems usually takes time and effort on your part. Continual training and reinforcement of lessons are the keys to success. But you can make a very good start in just a few days—and you may be surprised at just how much your dog improves.

What can you expect to achieve?

Given a fit, healthy adult dog of average intelligence (a Labrador retriever, for example) with no behavioral hang-ups, you can expect to achieve an obedience requirement described in the "Continuing Education" section in as little as two days—and there's a very good chance of achieving more. To attain this, you need to set aside approximately eight 15-minute sessions per day for two consecutive days. Your dog will need to rest for at least 45 minutes between sessions. Continually reinforce what you have initially taught throughout the week while out for regular exercise or in ordinary playtime in the yard.

Remember that some areas will need groundwork before you can achieve the desired response. For example, a dog who doesn't know his name is unlikely to come when you call him.

There are few things more relaxing and restorative than returning home from a hard day's work and receiving an ecstatic welcome, then taking your dog out to play to relieve your mental strain and physical aches. If only our relationships with other people were so simple!

TRAINER'S TIP

Ten to 15 minutes of concentrated training in a one-hour period is the maximum most dogs can cope with mentally and physically. Although dog training classes run for an hour or so, there are usually about six dogs involved, meaning that the trainer spends about 10 minutes working with each dog.

WHY YOU NEED A WELL-TRAINED PET

An untrained dog can be a real nuisance—a hazard to himself, his owner, and other people and animals. Owning an undisciplined pet can result in:

- Visitors no longer wanting to call for fear of being jumped on and covered with hair and slobber.
- Injury to you at home or on walks due to your dog's barging into you, pulling you along, or being aggressive.
- Injury to someone else caused by your unleashed dog ignoring your recall commands and attacking or chasing them, or by the dog running into the street and causing a traffic accident.
- Your dog being hurt or killed by a car.
- Legal action against you for damage caused by your dog.
- Damage to your home.
- Stress for you as well as for your dog.

How long should training sessions last?

This depends on a number of things:
- The age of your dog
- His type/breed (some have more aptitude for learning than others)
- His fitness and health

Puppies do not have long attention spans. Three 10-minute sessions a day for, say, collar and leash training, are far better than one 30-minute session, where the puppy's attention would wander. This is because the chances of finishing the session on a positive note are greater when you have the puppy's full attention.

Training periods are also dictated by the results you get: If, for example, you have allowed 10 minutes to teach your dog how to sit on command and he does it in 2, then finish on that positive note. The dog will remember this and be more receptive at the next training session.

Read and digest

As you read this book, you will see what order the training should follow; in addition, you'll learn how to understand and correctly relate to your dog—which is essential if you are to train him effectively—and how to apply the principles of no-fuss, commonsense training.

If you can only commit yourself to, say, two 15-minute sessions a week with no continual training in between, but you still expect your pet to be well-behaved and punish him when he does something unacceptable to you, the question you must ask yourself is "Should I have a dog?"

Mark your progress

Keep a diary of your dog's training progress: Write down what areas need improving, how long the training session lasted, and how he responded to your teaching methods. Note both positive and negative aspects. Not only will this be a valuable reference, it will also help a dog trainer or canine behaviorist assess both of you should you need to enlist help—particularly where behavior problems are concerned.

Keep it fun

The key point to remember when training, whether it is for 5 minutes or 15, is to keep it fun. This way the dog is more likely to remain focused on, and therefore responsive to, you. And you'll both enjoy yourselves—which, after all, is the whole point of having a dog.

Are you ready to become a dog owner?

The question to ask yourself is "I want a dog, but would a dog want me as his owner?" Successful relationships are based on positive two-way communication and respect, and you'll find that understanding how your dog thinks helps you to establish a more mutually rewarding partnership with him.

In this book, you will learn how to become a fair and positive leader and how to be clear, consistent, and respectful in all of your interactions with your dog. Then you'll be able to define a code of practice and behavior that he understands and will respond to in the way that you wish.

Having some idea of how a dog thinks and feels goes a long way toward achieving success in training him. The more you learn about the subject, the more you will accomplish.

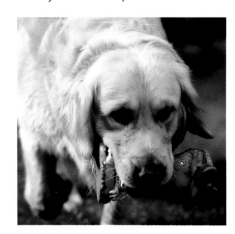

Equipment

Buying suitable equipment from the start helps to make caring for and training your dog easier, and this topic is covered in detail on pages 30–33 to help you avoid expensive mistakes. For example, you'd be surprised at what a difference it makes if you have a leash that is the correct length for the size of your dog!

Early learning

By following the clear instructions provided on pages 34–53, you will be able to guide and train your new puppy so that he grows up to be a well-mannered adult of whom you can be proud.

This section also describes many aspects of dog ownership, some of which you may never previously have thought about. If you are a prospective owner, you should consider all of them carefully before taking the plunge and acquiring a dog, for both your own and the animal's sake.

Continuing education

Successful training is based upon the simple principle of reward. Generally, dogs love to please their owners, and they enjoy doing so even more when they are rewarded for it. Reward-based training is, therefore, the key to having a happy and obedient dog. Food is an all-important aspect of a dog's life, so using food rewards is likely to achieve the training results you want. Using reward training in a variety of situations is explained in detail on pages 54–85.

Corrective training

Knowing why dogs "misbehave" will enable you to find solutions to specific problems. The case histories in this section describe just how effectively the methods outlined in the book work in practice.

Adopting a dog

Many people like the idea of adopting a homeless dog (see pages 28–29), but the reality of living with one can be very different from what you imagined. Behavior problems can and often do arise when the owner is ill-prepared for a dog whose past experiences and behavior are unknown. However, when you get it right, the rewards for both owner and pet can be great.

TRAINER'S TIP

Where canines are concerned, the pack instinct prevails. With this in mind, you must ensure that *you*, not your dog, are the leader of your particular "pack."

Food training—teaching your dog to sit, stay, and wait before he is given his food and then to wait for permission to eat—is a good start in achieving obedience in all other areas. Learn how to food train correctly and then how to use this principle as a fast and effective route to a well-behaved dog.

HOW TO BE THE PERFECT DOG OWNER

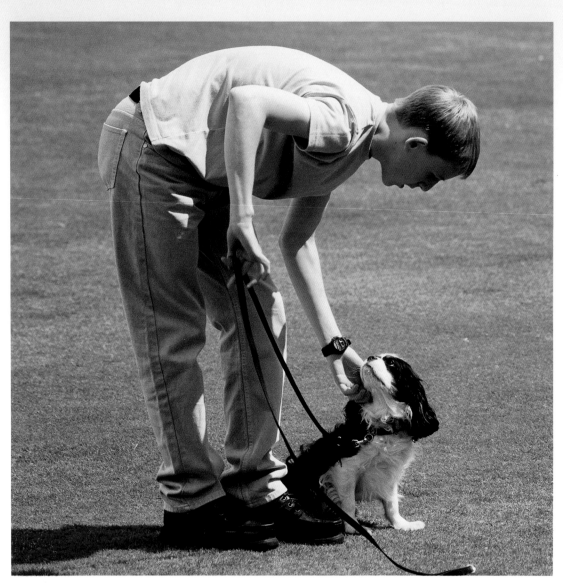

So you have always wanted a dog. Well, it's easy enough to go out and get one; the harder part is caring for him correctly.

If you have never owned a dog, you may find that having a well-behaved pet isn't as simple as you had imagined. There is more to looking after your pet than giving him a bowl of food once a day, taking him for a walk around the block, and spending 10 minutes or so throwing a ball for him to chase and retrieve. But help is at hand with this book!

Even if you have experience with dogs (perhaps your family had one when you were a child), the reality of having your own dog can be quite a shock when you discover exactly what's involved in caring for him. The first step toward having a dog you can enjoy and be proud of is to learn how to become the perfect owner—the following pages will teach you exactly what you need to know.

An ideal owner is one who trains his pet to be a "good citizen"—obedient, good-natured, and a pleasure to own.

A dog is for life

By now it should be clear that dogs are not simply consumable items that you can bring home to fit neatly into your life and provide you with comfort and entertainment, with no inconvenience to you. Dog ownership is richly rewarding if you do it right but thoroughly miserable for all concerned if you don't.

Before you set out to find a four-legged friend to share your life, there are some important things you must consider to ensure that you will be the owner every dog deserves.

Choosing the right dog

You should choose a breed and type of dog based on the environment you can offer him. There are several extremely important factors to take into account.

Your lifestyle • Some dogs dislike being left "home alone" while their owners are at work, and they can suffer separation anxiety. This can lead to behavior problems, such as house soiling, barking, and chewing.

Your living situation • Ideally, you should live in a house large enough to accommodate your family and your chosen size and type of dog, with plenty of space for everyone to enjoy. If you don't

Along with feeding, handling, and training your pet correctly, make sure you set aside plenty of time every day for the most important activity: having some fun together.

have a yard large enough for exercising your dog adequately, try to provide him with two long walks per day. If possible, include some playtime in an area where he can be safely off-leash.

If you are house-proud, you must be prepared for a lot of extra work to keep your home sweet-smelling and free of dog hair and muddy paw prints. For minimal mess and stress for all concerned, don't choose a large, hairy, slobbery type of dog.

Can you afford a dog?

The average dog lives for about 12 years, which is a long time to commit mentally, physically, and financially to another being. Apart from the initial expenses of buying or adopting your dog, spaying or neutering, and the essential equipment you will need, regular financial outlays include:

- Food

- Veterinary checkups

- Routine vaccinations

- Internal and external parasite treatments

- Vacation boarding fees

- Health and third-party/public liability insurance, if available

- Training classes

- Replacment equipment when necessary

- Specialized grooming care for dogs with certain types of coats

Your temperament • Since dogs can sense human emotions, a stressed owner is likely to end up with a stressed pet. Dogs respond best to calm, consistent handling. Shouting at or hitting your pet will confuse and frighten him, resulting in behavior problems. You need to be patient and controlled enough not to become angry if your dog does something undesirable.

Time • If you get a puppy, during the first couple of months you will need to spend a lot of time housebreaking and establishing basic obedience. Later, you'll need to allow at least two hours every day for care and exercise. Dog training classes—preferably weekly, but at least once a month—will help keep you both on the right track.

 Key points

An ideal dog owner is:

- Consistent and clear with directions
- Patient
- Self-controlled
- Calm
- Fair
- Positive
- Understanding

INSURANCE

Veterinary treatment for a serious injury or illness can be very expensive, so you may want to consider purchasing health insurance for your dog. Ask your vet for recommendations, then shop around for the best deal and be sure to read the small print on any policy proposals. Also, check with your own insurance carrier about options for liability coverage in the event of damage or injury caused by your dog.

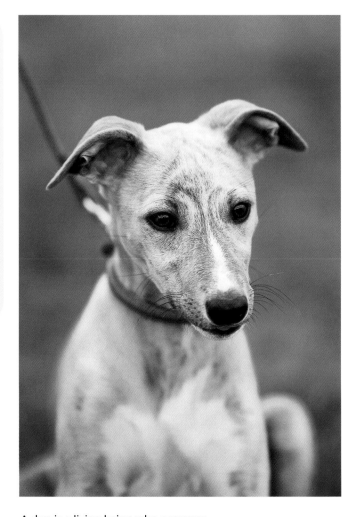

A dog is a living being who possesses feelings, a mind of his own, and a "language" that you must learn to understand in order to communicate with him effectively.

If there are children or young adults in the household, you must teach them to respect the dog and to handle and speak to him correctly. It's better to steer clear of the more naturally dominant breeds and choose one of the more gentle, equable types if you have children.

Case history: Choose your companion carefully

It's all too easy to fall for the first puppy you see, or a cute homeless dog whose eyes are begging you to adopt him. But pause to consider: After the acquisition of your "perfect pal," will the subsequent experience be as satisfying?

Just like humans, dogs are individuals, each with his own unique personality and behavior traits. To some extent, however, you can predict how certain breeds will behave and fit into your lifestyle—or not. The following story, which involves a traditionally bred outdoor hunting dog, is a prime example.

THE DOG • Penny, a two-year-old Jack Russell terrier, is "a wonderful little lady who is good with children and all other animals—and a great ratter." So said Penny's tearful owner, who was moving abroad and couldn't take the dog with her, to prospective new owner Karen. Once she was settled into her new home, it turned out that Penny was all of these things, but she was *not* a good house dog.

THE PROBLEM • Penny urinated and defecated in the house; in fact, she made a point of quite happily spending all day outside, coming in only to eat her meals, soil the carpet, and chew the furniture. Despite all efforts within her capabilities, Karen (a full-time working mother) couldn't cope. She simply hadn't the time or money to retrain this little outdoor dog into being an indoor pet.

THE SOLUTION • Karen looked for a suitable new home for Penny and finally succeeded when Jennifer answered her advertisement for "problem Jack Russell free to good home." Jennifer loved dogs. She was at home all day, wasn't house-proud, and could devote the time and energy necessary to care for and retrain a less-than-perfect pet successfully.

Recognize pack instincts

Dogs evolved as pack animals, and this instinct is still strong today. If you learn to understand canine instinct, how dogs "talk" to each other, and what their body language means, you will be better able to communicate with your dog.

Survival of the fittest

In any social group of animals, there has to be a pecking order, or chaos will ensue. In a canine pack, the dog who is mentally and physically strongest asserts himself as the leader, with the rest accepting their lesser roles and relying on the "boss" to provide for and protect them. Animal nature being what it is, however, there is always an element of competition for the prime position.

The instinct for self-preservation is strong. From day one, puppies strive for the best position at feeding time, with siblings pushing and shoving each other in their attempts to latch on to the nipples that produce the most milk. The strongest thrive; the weakest are lucky to survive.

At weaning, the most forceful pup gets the lion's share of any food mom brings back, but he has to eat quickly before the other pups gang up on him and steal his dinner. The pups also learn social skills from their peers, including how to socialize, behave, hunt, play, and fight. How well they learn these skills determines how well they integrate into the pack. As adults, the fastest, fittest, strongest, and most cunning dogs are better equipped to hunt for food as well as to guard their territory against possible intruders.

All of these instincts and characteristics are strong in domesticated dogs. A puppy's upbringing determines his character, so the better he is socialized with humans and accustomed to household living as a youngster, the better he will be able to deal with his future role as a canine companion to his human "pack."

If you take the time to understand how your dog's natural instincts affect his behavior and apply that knowledge to your training, you will establish a mutually rewarding relationship.

CHILD SAFETY

Never leave young children alone with a dog, no matter how good-natured or trustworthy you think the animal is. Often quite unintentionally, children can harass a dog unmercifully, until he can take no more and bites to warn them off (as he would an unruly pup in the pack). This is unacceptable in a human environment, so for everyone's sake, don't put the dog or children in a situation in which they are at risk.

Dogs are naturally sociable, but for an equable pack environment, there must be an appropriate hierarchy. The dog on the right is warning the other two not to enter his space, and they are deferring to his superiority.

Pack pluses

Living in a pack has many advantages. Hunting as a group means that:

• Food is easier to find and take.
• There is comfort, safety, and security in numbers.
• There are plenty of opportunities for play (for pure pleasure) and mock-fighting (practice for the real thing).
• There are many potential partners available to ensure perpetuation of the species.

☑ Key points

• Understand and work with your dog's natural instincts.

• Make him aware from day one that you are the pack leader, not him.

• Don't put the dog in situations in which his instincts may make him lash out and bite.

• Avoid attributing human characteristics to your dog.

Anthropomorphism

Many owners are unintentionally guilty of attributing human characteristics to their animals (anthropomorphism) to everyone's detriment. Examples of this include:

Attributing guilt

An owner may find that her dog has soiled in the house and say that the dog looked guilty because he knew he had done wrong. To a dog, however, defecating is just a natural function, so he has nothing about which to feel "guilty."

To uninformed humans, a dog's expression and body language may indicate that he knows he has done something wrong, when in fact he is displaying fear and/or submission in response to his owner's displeasure. However, he does not necessarily associate that displeasure with having made a mess on the floor!

Overfeeding

An owner may overfeed a dog or give him treats between meals because "he looks hungry." Instinctively, dogs are food-motivated (in the wild, they never know when their next meal will be), but if adequately fed, they are not hungry. If you fall victim to those pleading eyes, all you will do is allow your dog to train you in the art of room service and make him obese, thereby shortening his life.

Learn his body language

You can gauge the mental state of a dog from his posture and his facial and vocal expressions. As you get used to your own pet, you will learn his individual ways of communicating.

Generally, a stiff stance with jerky movements indicates aggression, uncertainty, and fear, while a relaxed posture and smooth movements mean the dog is at ease. A wagging tail does not always indicate a happy, friendly dog. You have to take into account the rest of his body language before deciding whether he is a friend or a foe. Look beyond the wagging tail and note the dog's hackles (the top of his shoulder, just behind his neck), his body stance, and his facial expression.

Calm and alert
The pricked ears and kind, interested expression indicate a **calm, content, and inquisitive** dog. This breed, the German shepherd, was developed in its native country to herd sheep, so its natural instincts are to guard and be watchful, and the expression here shows the breed at its best—alert, generous, and intelligent.

Reading body language

Wagging a raised, stiff tail	Implies tension and potential aggression
Wagging a low tail, possibly between the legs	Indicates fear and/or submission
Energetically wagging a tail at half-mast	Usually a good sign, generally implying neither tension nor depression
Wagging a tail with a relaxed body stance, "smiley" face, and lolling ears	Indicates a desire for play or kind attention
Hackles raised (hair standing up and bushed out), legs stiff, and eyes fixed	Indicates guardedness and readiness to attack if necessary

Here are two happy dogs with totally different personalities.

The young German shepherd (above) is energetic, curious, and always ready to play and investigate, while the mixed-breed (below) is much older, has a more laid-back and quiet personality, and is not as energetic.

Each displays a relaxed body stance and happy, kind facial expression in his own unique way. These examples demonstrate that knowing your own dog's personality is the key to being able to interpret his emotional state at any given moment.

Intense and watchful

This expression—the so-called collie eye—illustrates perfectly an **intense, watchful** dog, but not necessarily an aggressive one. A herding type, the Border collie was bred to manage sheep, and the instinct to herd (be it sheep, other animals, or people) is deeply ingrained. Such dogs are extremely intense in their emotional makeup and need careful and sympathetic handling to bring out the best in them. If you get it right, you'll have a fantastic companion; if you get it wrong, the dog will display all manner of behavioral "aberrations," and both dog and owner will be frustrated and miserable.

Frightened

This is a **fearful** dog. It is a pitiful sight, and one no owner should be proud to see. The stance indicates a browbeaten dog whose upbringing has been less than ideal. If a dog commonly displays this posture, he will need a great deal of confidence building in order to make him more emotionally stable and able to enjoy life.

✓ Key points

- Learning how to interpret your dog's body language will help you recognize his state of mind.

- Tail-wagging does not necessarily mean that a dog is friendly.

- A tense body indicates uncertainty, fear, or potential aggression, while a soft body stance and fluid movements indicate a relaxed, happy dog.

- A dog's natural instincts dictate his behavior, so you must take that into account as you work with your pet.

- Finding out about different breeds' inherent traits and using this knowledge when choosing a dog will help you find the right pet.

Unhappy or ill
This body posture indicates a **depressed and unhappy** dog. Such a stance could be due to a stressful atmosphere (a disruptive household or physical/mental abuse), or it could indicate physical discomfort due to illness.

Warning off/submissive
A classic example of **warning off** and **submission**. The dog on the right is displaying a "don't mess with me or I'll attack" stance, while the dog on the left is adopting an "okay, I'm backing off and won't bother you again" pose.

Recognizing illness

Some dogs are more stoic than others and will put up with considerable discomfort before their owners realize something is wrong. Despite a raging toothache, for example, some dogs do not whine or appear unwell, and it is only when the owner notices that the dog takes longer to eat or is not eating at all that a problem becomes apparent.

This is why it's essential to check your dog thoroughly every day for any unusual lumps or sore spots. Check his eyes, ears, and mouth for foreign bodies or any sign of inflammation, and watch for irregularities in behavior, eating, and elimination.

Aggressive

In **squaring up**, the dog on the left is displaying the attitude of being "armed to attack": His hackles are raised, and his body stance is tense, ready to propel him into defense against an apparently hostile approach from another. Yet dogs will attack with intent only if they deem it vital for their own well-being: In the wild, harming another pack member is always a last resort, because an incapacitated dog means that there is one fewer member available to guard and find food for the group as a whole.

Submissive

A **submissive** dog adopts this body posture. Crouching and licking his lips or yawning indicates "I'm insignificant, so please don't harm me!"

Understand his behavior

Dogs display a number of traits that we humans find strange or even disgusting (eating feces is a prime example). Yet dogs do what they do for a reason. As far as they are concerned, they're doing nothing wrong, and they become confused when we chastize them for doing something that comes naturally.

Knowing why dogs display certain behaviors enables owners to cope better with them as they occur. Don't get cross with your dog; instead, prevent him from doing potentially harmful things by distracting him with a game or toy or by avoiding difficult situations.

Eating grass
Eating grass aids your dog's digestion. When we get indigestion, we take an antacid; when dogs feel nauseated, they eat grass to induce vomiting and rid their stomachs of whatever ails them. Excessive grass eating, however, should be investigated by a vet.

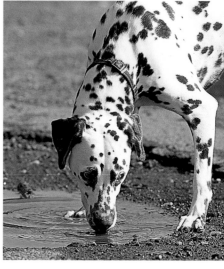

Inappropriate drinking
Some dogs seem to love **drinking from dirty puddles** or even slime-covered ponds, much to their owners' horror. It's not wise to let your dog do this, because the water could be polluted with chemicals or harbor parasites. And take care when preparing your car for winter. Dogs seem to find spilled antifreeze irresistible, but it is a deadly poison for them.

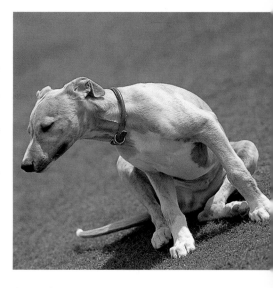

That's mine!
Guarding food or a toy by growling or snapping at anyone who approaches to take it away is a dog's way of saying "This is mine, and you can't have it." This line of defense is inappropriate in a human environment, and you must teach your dog from an early age to relinquish items without a fuss.

Scent communication
Sniffing the ground and other dogs' backsides and faces is a very important part of canine communication. By sniffing the ground, dogs can identify territorial boundaries and mating possibilities, while sniffing another dog's rear end identifies its sex and whether it is a potential friend or foe. Dogs sniff at human crotches for the same reasons.

Scooting
When a dog scrapes his bottom along the ground, propelling himself forward with his forelegs, this **"scooting"** action indicates that he is having discomfort in his anal area. This could be due to worms, blocked anal glands, constipation, or soreness. Such behavior requires veterinary attention to determine the cause and provide a solution.

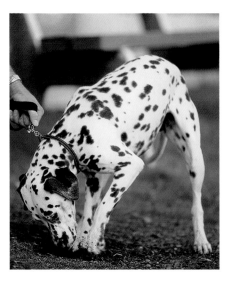

Possessiveness

Instinct dictates that to let another take away food will result in hunger. This principle of **possession** extends to toys and other items that a dog has: To give them up is a sign of weakness. Pet dogs should be taught from an early age to willingly relinquish items; otherwise, aggression problems may develop. It's fine to let a nonaggressive or nonpossessive dog occasionally win the toy in a tug game to keep his play motivation high, but make sure this is the exception rather than the rule.

Eating feces

Eating and rolling in other animals' feces is a canine habit that most owners find repulsive. To a dog, however, eating feces provides essential nutrients that his body is lacking, while rolling in them (and on dead animals) is a way of masking his own scent in preparation for hunting. See pages 104–105.

It's down here somewhere!

Digging indicates that a dog is looking for food or for quarry to chase, catch, and eat. Hunting dogs and terriers are particularly prone to digging in areas that their sense of smell tells them will be rewarding, so unless you want your yard rearranged, reserve a special area in which your dog can indulge in this harmless habit. If you bury a toy or bone in this special spot, your dog will get a reward for his efforts and keep returning there to try his luck again.

Other traits

Marking territory
Urinating against trees and defecating on or next to another dog's droppings is a highly effective "messaging service." The scent left behind tells other dogs who has passed that way, their sex, and their size (the reason some male dogs leave their excretions as high as possible).

Howling
This is the vocal signal that wild dogs use to call the pack together, which is why dogs left alone in a house may howl. It's their way of trying to make absent owners return to the fold. Being very social creatures, most dogs feel insecure and unhappy when they are alone.

Scratching grass
Scratching up grass with the front and back legs after urinating and defecating is a way of marking territory: Odors left by the scent glands in a dog's feet, along with the visual sign of disturbed earth, alert other animals to his presence in that area. Another possibility is that such scratching indicates relief at having finished emptying his bladder or bowels. There is an air of satisfied finality about this action, perhaps indicating that the dog no longer feels vulnerable to attack while relieving himself.

Pursuit
Chasing another animal in the wild is the first step in finding food or warning off intruders, so dogs find the experience very enjoyable and rewarding.

Respect his needs

In the same way that humans can, dogs can become stressed by the hectic pace of modern life. They don't go out to work like their owners, but they do have to put up with them rushing around in the morning and sometimes coming home tired and irritable at night.

Just as you respect human family members' feelings, you must consider how your behavior affects your dog. Whatever your emotional state, put that of your dog first. Being unselfish about fulfilling his mental and physical needs is the first step in respecting your pet.

Approach • Avoid sudden movements or loud noises directed at your dog, which he could construe as aggressive.

Reward • Dogs love to please, so always reward him for good behavior.

Food and drink • Always feed your dog a suitable diet in the correct daily quantity for his size and energy needs. Be sure he has a constant supply of fresh, clean water to drink.

Attention and exercise • Give your dog plenty of daily affection and playtime, sufficient exercise off-leash, and social interaction with other dogs.

Health care • Have your dog vaccinated against common diseases and treated as necessary for parasites such as fleas and ticks. Take him for veterinary attention whenever you think he may be ill.

Understanding • Don't reprimand your dog for displaying natural behaviors such as rolling in or eating other animals' droppings or sniffing under other dogs' tails. Simply distract him with a food treat or a toy.

Possessions • Provide your dog with toys to play with so he'll be less likely to take or chew other items in the house.

Companionship • Most dogs thrive in the company of humans. To deny them human companionship for long periods is unfair and can lead to problem behavior.

Elimination • Provide your dog with an area where he knows he can relieve himself, and always clean up after him.

Safety • Don't put your dog in situations that are hazardous or make him uncomfortable. Don't take him to places where there will be large crowds of people, for example, or where there may be uncontrolled, potentially aggressive dogs. Never leave him unattended in a car on a warm day, when heatstroke and suffocation are real risks.

TRAINER'S TIP

• Canine hearing is much more acute than that of humans. Loud noises, therefore, cause dogs discomfort and fear. Don't raise your voice in anger toward your dog or subject him to blaring music or loud volume from the television.

• Avoid prolonged eye contact with dogs; they perceive it as a threat.

• Make sure that everyone in the family sticks by the training rules. For example, if one person does not allow the dog on the furniture, another shouldn't encourage him to jump on the sofa.

• Don't allow games to become rough or encourage the dog to play-bite or jump all over you. Such games tend to get out of hand, with someone getting hurt, and the dog cannot understand why he is scolded for something he has just been encouraged to do.

☑ Key points

- Provide your dog with a place of his own where he can relax without being disturbed.

- Adhere to the training rules.

- Don't raise your voice in anger.

- Never use physical violence.

- Fulfill your dog's mental and physical needs.

Dogs are quick to sense their owners' emotions, and when all is not well, they can be upset.

Thus, your dog needs his own private space to retreat to and feel secure until he senses that you are in a good mood and ready to give him attention.

It can also be a place to escape from the children when he has had enough of play and to relax and sleep without being disturbed.

When petting your dog, be sure that you give him attention in a non-threatening way. The kind of petting shown here is only possible once you have built up a solid, trusting relationship with an even-tempered, placid dog.

Use command and reward

When training your dog, remember that he will learn to associate a word with an action, so you must be very aware of what your body as well as your voice is telling him. For example, if you are verbally trying to encourage the dog to come to you, make your body language as welcoming as your tone of voice.

Rewarding your dog every time he acts as you wish on a particular word-action command will lead to a learned response. Eventually, that response will become automatic every time you say the command and display the action, similar to the way that you would check your wrist if someone asked you the time.

Sit
One of the most useful commands to teach your dog is **"sit."** See pages 62–63.

Down
The **"down"** command is a natural progression from sit. See pages 64–65.

Most dogs will do anything for a tasty treat. Once you identify your pet's favorites, you'll have a great training tool. Interestingly, some dogs adore fresh fruit and vegetables such as apples, green vegetables, and tender young carrots, while almost every dog is partial to hot dogs and cooked liver. Some commercial treats are also very popular.

Keep some desirable toys aside so they have increased value as special rewards. When training, give your dog his favorite "high-value" toy for performing a required action, let him play with it for a few minutes, then take it away so it doesn't become ordinary.

If you use treats to reward your dog while training, be sure you have a supply in your pocket or a fanny pack and that they are chopped into tiny pieces; otherwise, your dog will get very fat very quickly.

"Rewarding" inappropriate behavior

Beware of unconsciously rewarding undesirable behavior, or your dog will assume that his inappropriate actions are acceptable. For example, don't let him push through a door in front of you; make him wait. If you let him through unchecked, the fact that he has gone out just as he wanted is a reward in itself.

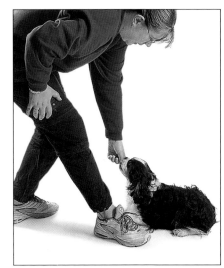

Stay
Sometimes a dog is uncomfortable with the "**stay**" command, but if taught correctly, he'll soon be happy to obey. See pages 66–67.

Here
Having your dog come to you when you command "**here**" is invaluable. See pages 76–77.

Good boy
Until your dog displays a learned response, you should reward each desired response to your commands. Thereafter, reward at random to keep his response levels high.

Commercial training aids

Training aids such as clickers, training discs, whistles, and remote or sound-activated liquid spray (not electric shock!) collars can be very effective in certain circumstances. But before using any of them, ask a trainer who is skilled in their use to show you how to use them correctly and effectively. Otherwise, you may end up confusing and/or frightening your pet.

☑ Key points

• Be consistent in your commands and actions. Always use the same words for commands so your dog doesn't get confused.

• Make sure that other family members use the same commands and actions that you are teaching him.

• Reward desired behavior with food, a toy, or attention, and your dog will learn more quickly.

• Give verbal commands in an encouraging and even tone of voice.

• Keep commands clear and well spaced (at least at first) so your dog can understand them.

• If your dog has learned to ignore a command and probably thinks it means something else, use a different word when you begin retraining.

Adopt wisely

A dog in an animal shelter is there for a reason; often, it's that someone couldn't cope with his behavior. He may be aggressive, not housebroken, destructive, or even all three. What makes you think you can cope with that dog when his previous owners couldn't?

When you adopt a dog, be prepared to give the animal as long as he needs to settle into his new home. Don't expect a miraculous change in his behavior overnight just because you are now his new owner. Be ready to work with him doing remedial training, which can sometimes take up to a year or more. Some dogs recover quickly from the traumas of their past experiences and adapt well to a new home, but many do not.

The right reasons

Many dog trainers have had people come to them complaining that the dog they have rescued from a shelter is misbehaving. It often turns out that they adopted the dog because they felt sorry for him or he looked cute or they were passing by, and once they had gone in, they just couldn't come out without one.

Dogs who have been mistreated or abandoned need time to recover from the treatment they have received and the way of life they have had to follow in order to survive.

☑ **Key points**

- Remember that shelter staff will be able to give you only limited information about dogs in their care.

- Be aware that many of the dog's behavior traits and his temperament will become apparent only after you get him home.

- Ask yourself if you're willing to invest time and money in training and remedial work, possibly for a prolonged period.

- Note that it's a good idea to discuss adopting a dog with a couple of trainers first.

- Think very carefully before committing yourself.

These are not the correct reasons for adopting a homeless dog, for you or the animal. The bottom line is that no matter what the dog looks like and no matter how sorry you feel for him, you and your family have to be able to live comfortably with him in your home.

While it's tempting to take the whole family to choose a dog, you should leave the children at home so their pleading doesn't influence your decision. Once you've seen a potential pet, ask the shelter staff about him and satisfy yourself that he will fit comfortably into your household. Then take the kids to meet the dog and see how they react to one another.

Case history: Rehabilitation

With correct training, it's perfectly possible to rehabilitate a "lost cause," as illustrated by this account of the vehicle chaser that follows below.

THE DOG • Mixed-breed Border collie Bruno was an animal shelter resident. A confirmed vehicle chaser, he had been there for about nine months, and at three years old, it was thought his behavior would never change.

THE PROBLEM • Bruno had a wonderful temperament and adored people. Several prospective owners had taken a real shine to him but were put off because as soon as he left the shelter and got anywhere near the street, he reverted to pulling on the leash and trying to attack cars as they passed.

THE SOLUTION • Keith Davis was asked to do some remedial work with Bruno so that he could find a home. First, Keith took him out into an enclosed exercise area to assess his general behavior and found that Bruno was a typical Border collie type: full of life and keen to play.

When Bruno was fitted with a headcollar and Check-Choke collar (see pages 41 and 59), with the leash clipped to both collars, there was an immediate improvement. Over the next three days, Keith spent an hour a day with Bruno at a set of traffic lights. First, he sat on a low wall, using favorite treats to keep Bruno's attention on him as traffic went by. Then, as the cars stopped at the lights, Keith walked Bruno up and down the street, then sat down again. After this, Keith gave a treat only when the dog was focused on him while traffic passed. Bruno soon got the idea: Chasing after traffic went unrewarded; not chasing traffic got him a treat!

By the third day, Bruno was content to sit and watch the traffic go by without leaping at it. At the same time, using the correct equipment resolved the pulling problem, and he was soon adopted.

Choose the right equipment

You will need to purchase a number of items in order to make life comfortable for both you and your dog.

Also called a den, pen, or cage, a **crate** serves as a bed and is useful for housebreaking, for keeping the dog separate from the family when necessary, and for safety when traveling with him.

Choose a **bed** that will be big enough for the dog when he is fully grown, made from a washable material and with raised sides to protect against drafts. **Bedding** should be thick enough for the dog to lie on comfortably and made from washable, quick-drying fabric.

Stainless steel or glazed ceramic **food and water bowls** are the most hygienic.

Buy a selection of durable **toys** for your dog, keeping some aside to use as special rewards.

Ask a trainer's advice on the most suitable **collar and leash** for your type of dog.

1 Fixed-length cord leash—not the preferred choice of most dog trainers, as it can't be lengthened or shortened as necessary.

2 Three-in-one medium-weight training leash—good for basic and intermediate training. It gives close control and allows the start of distance work, such as recall and stay.

3 Long training leash—training leashes are available in different lengths to suit your requirements; they are used for extended recall and stay exercises and for tracking exercises. They allow a dog freedom while retaining control, such as when there is livestock in the vicinity.

4 Three-quarter chain collar with adjustable leather strap—suitable for fully trained dogs. It's not suitable for training, as it lacks flexibility.

5 Check-Choke fabric collar with clip fastener—suitable for basic and subsequent training because of its flexibility and "kindness" (see Resources on page 126). If not available, use an ordinary leather or fabric collar.

Boredom-beater

A filled Kong toy will help keep your dog occupied when you are not there. You can also use it to distract him when necessary.

1 Fill the Kong with soft cheese or peanut butter. Push biscuit treats down into the soft filling.

2 Seal in the filling by smoothing it with a knife. Give the toy to your dog to enjoy!

Grooming gear

Smooth-coated dogs should be groomed with a hound glove—about 100 strokes from nose to tail, including the chest and sides, is usually adequate. Wipe around the eyes with a damp cotton ball, then a dry cotton ball. For an extra glossy coat, repeat the hound glove grooming with a towel and then a piece of chamois or velvet.

Terrier breeds should be groomed daily with a brush and wire glove in a similar manner to smooth-coated dogs.

Long-coated breeds should be groomed once or twice a week with a pure-bristle brush. If you find any knots or mats, sprinkle them with talcum powder and ease them out with your fingers. Be careful not to get powder in the dog's eyes, ears, or mouth.

If you're unsure of the best way to groom your dog, ask the advice of your vet or take the dog to a grooming parlor, where you can be shown the best way to look after his coat.

FIRST AID KIT

It's a good idea to have one on hand. Choose a kit that contains the following basic items:

✓ Saline solution
✓ Small bowl
✓ Small curved and blunt-tipped scissors
✓ Antiseptic cream
✓ Wipes
✓ Cold pack
✓ Self-sticking bandage
✓ Cotton-tipped swabs
✓ Cotton balls
✓ Surgical tape
✓ Tweezers

Activity toys and chews will keep your dog occupied. Give chews only when someone can supervise, in case of choking, and never give meat bones, which can splinter.

1 Durable rubber toy—designed for play and filling with treats.

2 Rubber treat ball—this design makes it even trickier to get the treats out.

3 Kong activity toy—almost indestructible; suitable for dogs with powerful jaws.

4 Bone-shaped biscuits—these come in different sizes to suit all dogs.

5 & 7 Meat-flavored soft chews—most dogs will do anything for these tasty treats.

6 Roasted pig ear—a great chew treat that also helps clean your dog's teeth.

8 Tough plastic, meat-impregnated chew—great for teething puppies.

9 Rawhide chew—these come in different thicknesses and help keep teeth clean.

Having your dog loose in the car is a hazard to the driver, the passengers, and the dog. When traveling with your dog, make sure he is safely secured by a **harness, crate or divider grill**.

A **see-through gate** is useful for keeping your dog out of certain areas of the house, but since it allows him to see his family, he won't feel isolated.

Case history: The right equipment

THE DOG • Troy was a boisterous 18-month-old German short-haired pointer. Sharon and Peter had intended to take him to training classes from the start, but they had put it off for various reasons.

THE PROBLEM • Sharon found that she couldn't handle Troy on walks; Peter was strong, but even he struggled to hold the dog.

THE SOLUTION • On assessing Troy at training class, Keith Davis saw that his collar and leash were made of heavy chain. Such weight is uncomfortable for a dog, and half the problem may have been that Troy was jumping about to try to relieve the pressure on his neck.

Keith fitted him with a headcollar, plus a Check-Choke collar for extra safety. Within 10 minutes, Troy was walking on the leash better than ever before. Sharon and Peter were asked to work on certain exercises and return to class the following week.

When they returned, Troy was back in his chain collar. Needless to say, he had again become uncontrollable. Keith told both owners to use the headcollar and Check-Choke when walking Troy. With correct use of the prescribed equipment, he quickly became a pleasure to take for walks.

EARLY LEARNING: From puppy to adult

Training plan

Week 1
- Teach the puppy to recognize and respond to his name.
- Begin socializing: Accustom the puppy to household sights and sounds—television, washing machine, vacuum cleaner, etc.
- Begin food training by handling the puppy while he is eating.
- Start housebreaking and crate training.

Week 2
- Begin collar and leash training.
- Have the puppy meet people of all ages and sexes. Remember to praise and reward where appropriate, not scold; simply ignore the pup if he displays inappropriate behavior.
- Begin any behavior training as necessary, such as for play-biting or jumping up.

Week 3
- Get the puppy used to seeing and being near other animals, including companion pets and larger animals such as cattle, if possible. For safety, keep him under control so he can't chase these animals.

Week 4
- Introduce car travel.
- Once he's been vaccinated, introduce the puppy to sights and sounds on walks; keep these short and close to home at first.

Week 5
- Gradually extend car trips.
- Start going to puppy training classes.
- By now, the pup will be going to his crate for time out or to rest in "his" den. If he is fully housebroken, you could replace it with a bed.

Congratulations—you have a puppy! Now you need to begin turning him into the ideal companion. The first few weeks of the puppy's life, while in the litter, laid the foundations. Now, correct training will set the standard of behavior you can come to expect as your puppy matures.

How good his manners will ultimately be depends on how well you teach him the social rules of living in a human environment. And you can start to set him on the right path in what will feel like no time at all!

Remember that puppies and young dogs need plenty of rest, just like babies and young children.

In the early months, avoid overexercising your puppy, as this can cause serious damage to his growing bones and developing muscles, tendons, and ligaments.

Once your cute little bundle of fluff is safely home and settled in, he will probably start getting you to run around after him—but only if you let him. While you need to be gentle and sympathetic toward your puppy, you also need to be quite strict; otherwise, you will soon find yourself exhausted by his demands.

What do I need to teach him?

In order to grow into amenable, housebroken, obedient, and well-mannered adults, puppies need to be taught how to be all of these things.

The training plan on the opposite page provides examples of the steps to take to start training. Detailed instructions about how to train puppies can be found in the following pages.

Remember to keep training sessions short— puppies have limited attention spans and get tired quickly. End sessions on a positive note, even if it means going back a step to do so.

✓ Key points

- Your puppy may begin teething at any time after you get him, so provide toys he can chew on for entertainment, comfort, and to help his adult teeth come through. Don't give him meat bones, as they can splinter and cause choking.

- Don't give your puppy an old slipper or shoe to play with, because this could lead to inappropriate chewing. He will simply view all footwear as items to be shredded.

- Don't use sticks or lumps of wood as playthings. Splinters can cause injury, and sticks have a nasty habit of spearing dogs. Invest in good-quality toys that are durable and safe; rubber Kongs are good choices.

1 Don't let your puppy demand attention any time he wants it. If he does, perhaps by jumping up or pawing at you, gently push him away.

2 Ignore him until he stops bothering you and remains quiet.

3 Then reward him for being quiet, patient, and undemanding. Through the use of reward, your puppy will learn that he gets attention when you want to give it, *not* when he demands it.

Sleep

For the first few weeks, your puppy's life will consist of eating and sleeping, intermingled with play. Although it is tempting to play endlessly with him, don't overtire the youngster in the early, stressful days when he is settling into his new home.

In his natural habitat, the puppy would regulate his own sleeping and waking times, so within reason, you should try to maintain that pattern. Give him a crate or bed in a quiet area of the house to which he can retreat and rest without being disturbed. Try to keep him active during the day so he'll sleep at night.

Try not to get up when the puppy cries during the night. If he gets you up the first time he cries, he will learn that this behavior gets attention—and you will be up every night!

Feeding

Your breeder should give you feeding instructions when you pick up your puppy, detailing the type of food he's being fed (this should be a puppy diet) and the daily quantity. As the puppy grows, consult your vet about the best diet for him.

Name training

1 One of the first things you will want to teach your puppy is to come to you when you call his name. Crouch down low and, in a warm tone and with an open gesture, call his name clearly and forcefully but without anger.

2 When the puppy comes to you, give him a treat and lavish praise. He'll soon learn that he is well rewarded for coming to you when called. It really is as simple as that!

Inspecting your puppy's belly

Dogs feel very vulnerable when exposing their bellies, so it's important to teach them from an early age that it is a rewarding experience. This way, you or your vet will be able to quickly and easily check injuries or look for ticks, whenever necessary.

1 You can use food treats as an incentive to teach your pup to lie down and roll onto his side so you can inspect his belly. Hold the treat where it will encourage the puppy to lie down—that is, down near the floor.

2 Move the treat over the puppy's shoulder so he moves his head to follow it.

3 When you have moved the treat far enough, the puppy will flop onto his side, belly up. At this point, give him the treat and simultaneously stroke his belly and praise him lavishly. Repeat the exercise and add a word command such as "belly" so the puppy learns what you want and will roll over automatically.

Handling

Your puppy must defer to you, his owner, or he will get the upper hand and be more difficult to handle as he gets older. Dogs generally dislike having their eyes, mouth, paws, ears, belly, and anal area inspected. However, you and your vet or dog groomer need to be able to touch and inspect these areas easily if they require attention. Handle your puppy from an early age, being as gentle as possible so the experience is not unpleasant.

Play training

If you turn training into a game, your puppy will respond wonderfully. Try to channel play with your puppy into what will later become recall and retrieve exercises. If he brings a toy to you and drops it or gives it to you, reward him. You can also use toys to gain your puppy's attention. Show him that if he wants the toy, he will have to work for it.

If your puppy spontaneously offers behaviors that you want, you can use the opportunity to further his training. For example, when he eliminates outside, be quick to praise and reward him; if he lies down beside you without pestering you for attention, reward him.

If taught gently but firmly early in his life, your puppy will let you handle all areas of his body without stress to either of you.

Health care

Just like a human baby, a puppy needs regular checkups and inoculations. Be sure to follow your vet's recommendations.

Vaccination • First inoculations are usually done when the puppy is eight weeks old; consult your vet about which vaccinations he will need and when they should be given. Thereafter, the dog should have yearly boosters.

Parasite control • Find out from the puppy's breeder when he was last wormed and treated for other parasites, so you can keep up with treatment in the early months. Your vet will supply the most suitable and effective treatments for internal and external parasites.

Neutering • There are good reasons for neutering or spaying pet dogs, including:

• Helping to promote a more equable and gentle disposition.
• Reducing susceptibility to some diseases. In some cases, neutering may become necessary for health reasons.
• Preventing unwanted pregnancies, therefore reducing the number of unwanted dogs.
• Helping to prevent roaming in male dogs and reduce aggressive tendencies in both sexes.

However, neutering is always something that should be discussed with a vet, taking into account each individual dog's character, health, and his position within the household pack if there is more than one dog involved.

☑ Key points

• Allow your puppy to settle into his new environment quietly; don't expect too much of him too soon.

• Make sure your puppy has a private area to which he can retreat and rest undisturbed whenever he wants.

• Puppies are very motivated by food, so treats are extremely useful training aids, as are toys, attention, and praise.

• Don't give in to attention-seeking behavior.

• Handle the puppy from day one to accustom him to being touched and inspected all over.

Carrying a puppy

1 Crouch down and gently but firmly gather the puppy to you as shown, with one arm around his chest to keep him from breaking free and the other arm under his bottom for support.

2 Stand up slowly, keeping the puppy close to your body so that he feels safe and secure and can't jump from your arms.

3 Carry the puppy close to your chest. To put him down, simply reverse the actions. Throughout, bend from the knees to avoid straining your back.

Collar and leash training

✔ Key points

- Walk the puppy on your left side with a slack leash; keeping it taut will encourage him to pull against or resist it.

- Keep sessions short and frequent, or the puppy will become bored and restless. Always finish on a positive note.

- Make training a game so the puppy will think it's fun, not a chore.

- Check collar fit regularly as your puppy grows.

- Once your puppy is leash trained, you can start attending puppy socialization classes.

You would think that walking a puppy on a leash is simple, wouldn't you? Just put on the collar and leash, and away you go. However, if these items are not introduced to him correctly, leash training can be difficult and traumatic for both you and your puppy.

Leash training

First, put the collar on the puppy for short periods, praising him lavishly as you do so. Then distract him with a game or treat so that he gets used to the feel of something around his neck and associates it with a pleasant experience.

Once your puppy is fully accustomed to wearing his collar, clip on a short leash and let him follow you around the house for short periods so he gets

1 Hold the leash in your right hand and a reward (a treat or favorite toy) in your left, moving it around to get the puppy interested in it.

2 Walk backward and call the puppy's name; keep the leash slack and entice him with the reward. If he is reluctant to follow, let him mouth the toy or give him a taste of the treat, call his name again, and continue backing away. He will be sure to come with you.

used to the feel of it attached to his collar. Again, be generous with praise and rewards while he is wearing it. Once he is completely happy with his collar and leash, you can start to teach your puppy to walk by your side while you are holding the leash.

Leading on the left

The reason for walking your puppy on your left, with the leash across your body and held in your right hand, is that most people are right-handed. This is the stronger side, so if the dog is walking on the left side and pulls forward, your body is better balanced to control the pull. In addition, the hand closest to the puppy is left free to hold a treat or toy and coax him as necessary.

The idea of using a Check-Choke collar (see Correct Equipment, at right) is to attract the puppy's attention with the rattling of the chain. When you use your right hand to check the puppy, you can pull the leash across your body and rattle the chain. If you held the leash on the same side as the puppy, you would pull against his body weight and choke him.

3 Once the puppy is happily walking toward you, bring the hand with the treat around toward your leg and then forward, and he will turn to follow it.

4 Walk forward, rewarding the puppy as you do. Use the commands "walk" and "heel" so that he learns to associate the actions with the command and reward.

5 Note the correct way to hold the leash and the correct position for the puppy by your side.

6 During initial leash training, keep a treat in your left hand so that if the puppy becomes distracted, lags behind, or starts pulling, you can entice him back to the correct position and pace, then reward him.

Correct equipment

COLLAR
Ideally, choose a "kind" training collar such as a Check-Choke (see Resources on page 126). This type of collar is designed so that when the puppy is checked, the chain rattles and gains his attention. It is *not* designed to cause uncomfortable tension around his tender neck. You can also use an ordinary leather or nylon collar but be sure that any collar you choose is the right length, weight, and width for your puppy. When it's fitted, you should be able to get two or three fingers underneath it: If too loose, it may slip off; if too tight, it will be uncomfortable, especially when the puppy is eating or drinking.

LEASH
Leash type is important. First, it must be comfortable for you to hold. Next, it must be of a suitable length to maintain slack tension. An adjustable nylon leash that can be lengthened or shortened will give you the best of both worlds.

Making new friends

Imagine a world where you can't speak the language, you are afraid of someone walking toward you on the street, or meeting a group of people terrifies you. Without realizing it, you can turn your dog into a nervous wreck by not socializing him correctly to make him ready for such situations.

It is during the sixth and seventh weeks of life that puppies in a litter learn the finer points of social skills in their family environment. Once you take your puppy home, you are responsible for introducing him into your world. This is the only way he can discover how to socialize with other

Handling your puppy while he's eating will help ensure that he doesn't become possessive about food. Adding more food to the bowl mid-meal teaches him that someone handling his food represents a reward, not a threat.

Accustom your puppy to meeting and being with people of all ages and both sexes, and reward him so that he views their company as a good thing.

☑ Key points

- Don't let your puppy jump up at people or allow them to let him do so. Give him attention only if he waits patiently to be petted.

- Introduce your puppy to household sights and sounds—such as the television, radio, washing machine, and so on—one at a time over a period of days so he is not overwhelmed.

- Get the puppy used to car travel as soon as possible, beginning with short trips, but make sure he is secure in the vehicle. It's best to put him in a crate with his blanket for comfort and a toy to distract him.

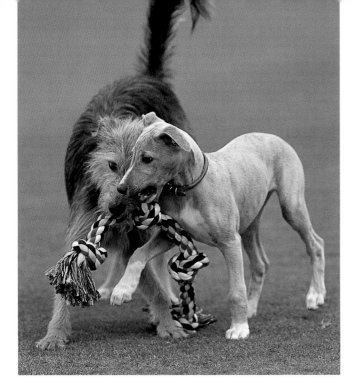

When introducing your puppy to older dogs, start with a good-natured one who will play with the youngster and not intimidate him.

TRAINER'S TIP

To help accustom a puppy to another animal in the household, put his bedding in with the other pet for a while to transfer its scent, then put the blanket back in the puppy's bed. He will learn to recognize the other pet's scent as familiar and comforting.

dogs successfully, be well-mannered when meeting people on the street, and learn when enough is enough during play.

Sights and sounds

Your puppy needs to become accustomed to traffic noise so he won't be frightened by it when you are walking him. Get him used to both day and night walking so he becomes oblivious to headlights as well as the noise and sight of vehicles.

If your puppy has a problem with this, find a quiet stretch of street where you can spend some time just sitting and watching the world go by. Each time a vehicle approaches, distract your puppy by showing him a treat, then when the vehicle has passed, let him have it. This way he will come to associate traffic with getting a reward.

Other animals

You also need to accustom your puppy to other animals, including cats, rabbits, guinea pigs, hamsters, caged birds, cattle, horses, sheep—in fact, anything to which you can introduce him. Again, use food rewards as a distraction if the puppy becomes excited or frightened. Then reward him for being quiet and calm when he is around other animals.

Puppy training classes

Once your puppy has been vaccinated, the best way to socialize him is to take him to puppy training classes held in a secure area. There he can meet other puppies of his own age and size, as well as other people.

When allowed to mingle—first on the leash, then loose—the puppies will quickly find an acceptable level of chase and play and sort out the pecking order among themselves. It's important in these initial stages that they are not forced into a frightening situation. A good trainer will ensure that play-fighting doesn't get out of hand and will prevent any bullying.

Crate training

Training your puppy to use a crate happily will come in very handy. Also known as a den, pen, or cage, a crate serves as a bed and a quiet, secure place to which your puppy can retreat. It also keeps the puppy (and later the adult dog) separate from people when necessary, is useful for housebreaking, and is a safe place to put him when traveling in a vehicle.

TRAINER'S TIP

Gradually increase the period of time for which the puppy is left in the crate while you are at home, from a few minutes to up to a half-hour. At four or five months of age and older, he will recognize it as a "safety zone" and happily stay there overnight or while you are at work.

A crate can be a great tool for housebreaking, but remember that you should leave the puppy in the crate for extended periods only after he has eaten and been outside to exercise and take care of bathroom needs. Since dogs dislike soiling in or near their beds, having to relieve himself in the crate could make your puppy unwilling to stay inside it.

It's important to introduce your puppy to a crate correctly, or he may view it as a prison rather than a pleasant, safe place to be.

To start, use toys and treats to encourage your puppy to go into the crate, leaving the door open so he can go in and out as he wants. Put the crate in a quiet but not isolated area of the house so the puppy won't be disturbed when he's inside but at the same time will not feel abandoned. Be careful not to place it in direct sunlight or in areas that get too hot or too cold.

Crates come in all sizes, with various types of openings. Choose one that will be big enough for your puppy when he is fully grown. A two-door foldaway crate is especially convenient for use in a vehicle. Put comfy, familiar bedding and the puppy's favorite toys in the crate to encourage him to go inside and feel at home. The best time to do this initially is after a play session, when he is tired and ready for a rest.

Accustom the puppy to going in and staying in the crate by feeding him there, but with the door open at first so he doesn't feel trapped. Once he is used to this and willingly goes in at mealtimes, feed him with the door closed for short periods, then gradually extend the time. Remember, though, that puppies generally need to relieve themselves after eating, so he will have to go outside soon.

Help the puppy learn that the crate is a nice place to be by giving him a filled activity toy such as a stuffed Kong (see page 31), which will keep him pleasurably occupied.

☑ Key points

- Never use a crate as a "punishment pen."

- Crates made of plastic-covered metal are quieter and easier to clean than those made of bare or galvanized metal.

- To give the puppy extra privacy or encourage him to be quiet (provided he isn't crying to go outside), cover the crate with a blanket.

- You can use a crate as a portable kennel when visiting or on vacation. For safety, you can keep your puppy in the crate when introducing him to other household pets.

- Once he is used to a crate, a puppy who is prone to chewing furniture, carpets, and other inappropriate objects can be removed from temptation until the behavior has been corrected.

Housebreaking

Puppies need to be taught appropriate bathroom habits; they *do not* learn them automatically. You can expect a few accidents at first, so keep your pup in areas where it doesn't matter if he deposits the odd pile or puddle.

Be prepared at first to take your puppy for lots of outside visits at the appropriate times. Just like human babies, young dogs need to relieve themselves quite frequently until they gain fuller control over their natural bodily functions.

☑ Key points

- Don't expect a young puppy to be clean in the house overnight or throughout the day if shut inside. If you do catch him in the act, pick him up and take him outside to the bathroom area.

- Never shout at or smack your puppy if he has an accident; he won't understand why you're angry and will simply become frightened of you.

- Never rub a puppy's nose in his mess in the belief that this will stop him from soiling in the house.

- Praise and reward lavishly when the puppy relieves himself outside so he learns that it's well worth repeating.

- Always take the puppy outside after waking, eating, and playing.

- After eating and going outside, the longest a young puppy can be left in a crate during the day is three to four hours; at night, he should be confined for no more than five to six hours. In any case, leaving a puppy in a crate longer than this is very unfair.

- You must learn to recognize the signals when your puppy needs to relieve himself. He may pace the floor, refuse to settle, or whine and go to the door. Sometimes puppies will seek a private place to go, such as behind furniture, so be watchful for this.

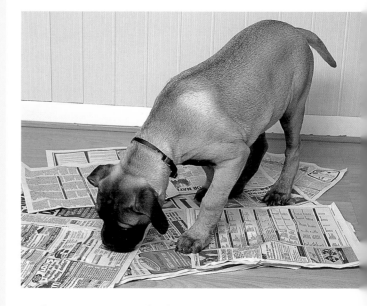

Until your puppy is completely housebroken, it's a good idea to put down newspaper in the area he inhabits so that messes are easier to clean up.

Teaching appropriate habits

1 A puppy usually needs to relieve himself after eating and playing, so these are the times to take him outside to his designated bathroom area, which should be marked off with a length of rope or hose to define it clearly.

2 Wait until the puppy relieves himself, then praise him so he knows that his actions in that place were desirable.

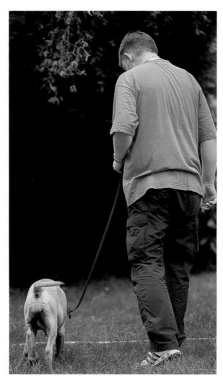

3 Leaving the puppy's last droppings will indicate to him by sight and smell that this is the right place to go.

Using crate training

Crate training (see pages 44–45) comes in handy when housebreaking your puppy, but don't leave a young pup in a crate all day or night and expect him to be clean. He won't be able to contain himself and will end up distressed because he's soiled his bed. You must be able to take your puppy out to relieve himself at regular intervals or arrange for someone else to do so.

TRAINER'S TIP

Your puppy will almost certainly need to relieve himself after he wakes up, so this is another good time to take him outside.

Cleaning up

Accidents do happen. When cleaning up feces, urine, or vomit, avoid using household cleaners that contain ammonia, a component of excretions. The lingering smell will encourage the puppy to soil the same spot again.

Instead, use commercial pet-stain cleaners (available at pet stores) on soiled areas in the house. These products eliminate odors so your puppy won't be attracted to the same spot again.

No biting!

Puppies love to bite and chew things because it helps them teethe. In addition, play-biting or fighting is part of the instinctive canine learning process for hunting, food-gathering, and establishing status in the pack.

Your puppy will treat you like a pack member while he is learning social skills, but you must help teach him (just as his mother would) exactly what constitutes appropriate and inappropriate behavior. Play-biting is definitely inappropriate.

If encouraged or left unchecked, play-biting becomes increasingly severe, until the dog is of a size and age where he really hurts and frightens human "targets," especially children. You must teach your puppy that biting is unacceptable.

☑ Key points

- Instead of your hand or arm, give the puppy toys that he can chew and play with without harming anyone.

- Yelp loudly if the puppy tries to bite you. Move away from him and ignore him until he leaves you alone, then reward him with attention for not biting. This imitates the actions his mother and littermates would take to discourage rough play.

- Don't encourage the puppy to play-bite, and be very strict about not allowing children to let him bite them when they are playing together.

- Don't tap the puppy's nose when he bites; it will just encourage him to continue biting.

- Handle your puppy's mouth from day one so he becomes accustomed to hands being around his jaws without thinking they are something to bite. Praise the puppy for letting you do this, so he learns that he's rewarded for not biting.

Discouraging biting

1 Spray a nontoxic, bitter-tasting liquid (available at pet stores) on the areas of your body that the puppy frequently tries to bite—usually hands and arms.

2 Hold out your hand and let the puppy mouth it.

3 The puppy will usually recoil in disgust at the foul taste. After a number of repetitions, he'll learn that biting humans is unpleasant.

TRAINER'S TIP

You can use repellent spray for pets to discourage your puppy from chewing on household items, such as table legs and shoes.

A noisy deterrent

Puppies don't like loud or sudden noises, so you can use such sounds to discourage play-biting.

1 Half-fill a small tight-lidded container with pebbles and shake it hard when the puppy tries to bite you.

2 He'll react in surprise at the noise and back away from you.

3 When he does, leave him for a moment to settle down, then go to him and give him attention. This way, he learns that biting results in an unpleasant shock, while not biting is rewarded.

Stay down!

In the wild, dogs instinctively greet returning pack members by sniffing and licking at their mouths to try to get them to regurgitate or drop food.

Since the mouth and face represent a rewarding area of the body, puppies jump up at us in an attempt to reach it. We must teach them that this is not rewarding, so never respond to your puppy when he jumps up.

Although a little puppy jumping into your arms may seem truly adorable, just imagine how you would cope with such behavior if he were fully grown. Even if you don't mind him almost knocking you over as he plants two muddy paws on your shoulders, he could pose a real danger to other people, such as pregnant women, frail or elderly people, and children when out on walks.

Training him to stay down

1 If your puppy jumps up at someone, tell her to fold her arms so that they are out of his reach, turn away to avoid eye contact, and ignore his actions.

☑ Key points

- Most people, especially children, love to say hello to puppies (and adult dogs) when out walking, but it's important that you ask them not to do so until the puppy sits and waits quietly for attention.

- Always ignore the puppy when he jumps up.

- When the pup is trying to get attention, avoid eye contact and acknowledge him only when he has settled down and has all four paws on the ground.

- Give the puppy attention only if you have first called him to you.

- When you are finished petting him, say "enough" and gently push him away, fold your arms, avoid eye contact, and ignore him.

- Play with the puppy only if you initiate the contact. Let him know when you are finished, as described above.

- Make sure visitors know and follow your rules for giving the pup attention, and tell them what to do if he jumps up at them.

2 The person should continue to ignore the puppy until he stays down, which he will eventually do when he doesn't get a reaction.

3 She should wait until the puppy settles down and makes no further attempt to approach or jump up.

4 Now the person should reward the puppy with attention and praise. This teaches him that jumping up is a negative experience, while not doing so is a positive one.

5 Practice this exercise at home and out on walks until your puppy makes no attempt to seek attention or jump up at someone who approaches him. Only then should the person acknowledge the puppy.

TRAINER'S **TIP**

It's not fair to allow your dog to jump up at you as a puppy and then scold him for doing so when he grows into a big dog. He will be confused by your inconsistent reactions.

Food training

Food is very important to dogs, and they can become possessive about it. In the litter, puppies fight over the best teat in order to get as much food as their bellies will hold, and they do the same with solid food after weaning. This behavior is relates to their experience in the wild of never knowing when their next meal will be or where it will come from.

Establishing pack hierarchy

In the pack, the highest-ranking members eat first, then allow the lower-ranking ones to feed. This rule must also apply in your household, or your puppy will assert himself as number one—and not just at mealtimes!

You need to teach your puppy that he doesn't have to fight for food and that a human near his food bowl isn't a threat to his meal. You must also assert yourself as pack leader so the puppy eats when you want.

Permission to eat

1 Have your puppy on the leash and put down his food bowl. Don't allow him to eat, using the leash to restrain him as necessary, along with the command "leave." Encourage him to sit, or at least stand, quietly by your side.

2 Wait until the puppy looks at you for permission to eat, although this may take a while. Eventually, he will realize that you are in control, and he'll want to see if you are ready to let him eat.

3 When he does this, say "eat" and allow him to do so. Praise him for his patience.

4 As the puppy is eating, add a treat or two to the bowl so that he views hands near his food as nonthreatening.

- If there are children in the household, show them how to do food training so the puppy also views them as being of higher rank.

- Do the food-training exercise at every meal until the puppy waits off-leash to be told to eat.

- Once the puppy learns to associate the "leave" command with leaving food alone until he's permitted to have it, you can use the command for other things, such as items that he chews.

- While the puppy is waiting to eat, move away from him and use the command "stay," which he'll do because he's unwilling to leave the food. Then return to the puppy, praise him, and allow him to eat.

CONTINUING EDUCATION:
The well-mannered dog

Training plan

Week 1	Sit
	Lie down
	Roll over
	Stay
Week 2	Socialization
	House manners
Week 3	Away
	Retrieve
	Recall

The key to owning an obedient, well-trained dog is to start him on the right track when he is a puppy. But what if you acquire an adult dog who wasn't properly trained as a puppy and whose manners leave something to be desired?

Training adult dogs

Choose the area(s) of obedience that you would most like to improve, either from choice or necessity, and work on those first. However, bear in mind that if you want to improve, say, recall, your dog must already know his name; if he doesn't, you will need to teach him this first. The same applies for street safety—if your dog is not used to being on a leash or has no leash manners, you will have to work on this as the first step.

All areas of obedience training require continual reinforcement to ensure that both you and your dog stay sharp. See the step-by-step instructions for teaching these exercises in the following pages.

Some areas of training may be started at the same time, as they naturally complement each other. Three groups of such related areas are:
- Sit, lie down, roll over, and stay
- Socializing and house manners
- Away, retrieve, and recall

Otherwise, try to initiate training in separate weeks to avoid confusing your dog.

The training plan above is an example of what can be achieved in three weeks of training, starting with eight 10- to 15-minute training sessions per day for the first two days, plus continual reinforcement of all exercises during daily walks and playtime for the following five days. It is based on a fit, healthy adult dog of average intelligence who has no behavior problems and already knows his name.

Work out a plan based on your dog's needs for a maximum of 10 to 15 minutes of concentrated training in a one-hour period, plus additional play/exercise time for light relief and fun. Break the areas of obedience training you want to work on into a progressive program, moving on to the

✔ Key points

- Some dogs take longer than others to grasp what you are trying to teach.

- Being patient and staying relaxed reap rewards.

- Remember: Little and often is best. Keep training sessions short, and always finish on a positive note.

- Reward all desirable behaviors.

- Attending regular training sessions will be beneficial for you and your dog.

- A key element that forms the base for all training is food control. The method used to food train adult dogs is exactly the same as that used for puppies: Follow the procedure given on pages 52–53.
- You don't want to reward with food treats forever, though, because your dog may become fat. Once he understands what you want, you should give food rewards only intermittently. At other times, give lavish verbal and physical praise, which your dog will appreciate just as much.

With time and correct training, developing a well-mannered dog is not as difficult as you may think.

next stage only when you have achieved the results you require in the current stage.

Good manners

The following pages explain how you can train your adult dog in the basics of good manners, from walking to heel on the leash and coming to you when you call him, to sitting, staying, and behaving well in the house.

Some people take these things for granted, expecting a dog to know automatically what is required of him, but that simply isn't the case. You wouldn't expect a new employee to know the job on the first day, and it's the same for a new dog. He has to get to know you and your way of doing things, while you have to get to know him and find out what makes him tick.

Food rewards and praise are the most effective ways to get a favorable response. Rewarding desired behaviors will soon have your dog behaving the way you want him to.

Good instruction

Keep a diary so you can see how things are going, and note areas of particular success or difficulty so you can work on the exercises that your dog finds more challenging. Above all, stay calm, be patient, and make training fun.

Finding a good trainer will be invaluable in helping you turn your dog into a well-mannered companion. Regular training sessions will help point you in the right direction, and both you and your dog will enjoy them. Many trainers will also give you the chance to try various activities such as agility, flyball, scenting work, and the increasingly popular heel work to music.

So, although this book shows you how to go· about things the right way, remember that additional on-the-spot help and advice can be invaluable when it comes to putting what you've learned into practice.

All dogs are different

Some dogs learn faster than others. Large breeds tend to mature more slowly, so you need to be extra patient with them. Small dogs, on the other hand, can be too clever for their own good, and you will have to be on your toes!

Bear in mind that working breeds, while intelligent, have an inbred instinct to chase and retrieve, guard, or herd—or all three—so they require disciplined handling and training to get the very best from them. Some owners may find such dogs too much of a handful.

If you own a dog like this and really cannot commit to or give him the type of training and exercise he needs, you need to consider your options. Finding the dog a home with someone who can offer the type of environment and training he needs is not a failure on your part. Rather, it is a selfless act that will give the dog a chance to lead a more fulfilled and happier life.

Name response

If you acquire your dog as an adult, he is likely to already have a name, to which he may or may not respond. If he has learned that responding to his name is unrewarding, you have two choices: Change his name to one you prefer and teach him to respond to it, or retrain him to respond to his existing name.

When choosing a name, pick one that's short and rolls off your tongue in one or two syllables. This way, it is easy to say quickly, and the dog will soon learn to recognize it. Beyond this, naming your dog is a matter of personal choice.

Homework

Once you have brought your new dog home from the animal shelter or his previous owner's home, you will need to start from the beginning. Don't assume that the dog is aware of his name or that he is used to being called by it.

Let your dog find his way around his new home. Once he has investigated his surroundings, you can start to ask him to come to you. Call him by his name and add the command "come." When the dog reacts to your voice, entice him to you with encouraging words, and as he reaches you, give him a treat or praise. Initially, try to attract the dog's attention by calling him; if this fails, you can revert to treat training. You can also add treat training to speed up the learning process.

Teaching your dog his name

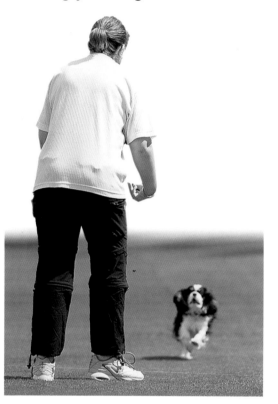

1 When you begin name training, work in a secure area so the dog can't escape your control, or have him on a long leash. Open your arms to indicate a friendly welcome and call the dog's name enthusiastically to get his attention.

2 As your dog looks at you, offer a tasty treat that he can't resist, or his favorite toy.

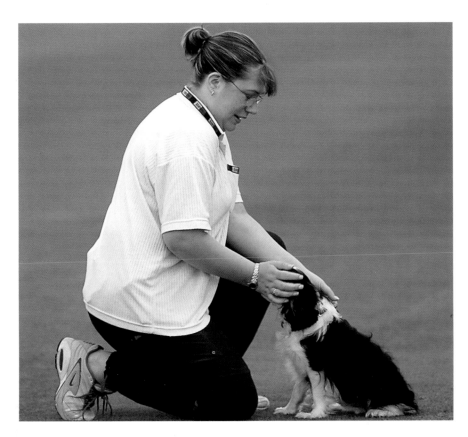

3 Call the dog again and crouch down so that you don't appear intimidating, especially to a small or nervous dog. When he comes to you, give him a treat or toy and praise him lavishly. With this method, your dog will learn that coming to you when you call his name is very rewarding.

☑ Key points

- Don't always put your dog on the leash when he comes to you in response to his name. Instead, play with his collar and handle his neck. Then release him with the command "away" or "go play." Repeat this exercise often so the dog associates coming to you with play, not with loss of freedom.

- Remember that your dog's name is just that: It's *not* a command. Many people shout the dog's name and expect him to sit or to walk with them without a command. Your dog can only do what you ask him to do, so tell him what you want.

- Always remain calm when calling your dog. If he doesn't respond, ask yourself if he actually knows what you want. Have you demonstrated things clearly enough for him to understand?

- If the dog doesn't respond to his name, stop, take a break, and try again later. Never call his name in anger; he'll be unlikely to come to you if he generally associates that tone with an unpleasant experience.

Leash manners

Taking your dog for a walk is pleasant and relaxing for both of you—if he is leash trained correctly. If your dog isn't accustomed to a collar or leash, turn to pages 40–41 for advice on how to get started.

One common problem is the dog walking ahead or even pulling his owner along in his eagerness to get on with the walk and reach wherever he is going.

Conversely, the dog may lag behind or need to be dragged away from a patch of grass he is intent on sniffing.

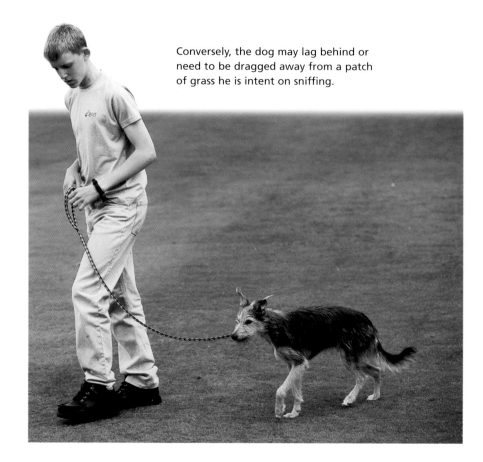

TRAINER'S TIP

If you use a retractable leash, it's essential to check it regularly to be sure it's in good working order. Also, the leash should be able to take the weight of your dog if he bolts and you have to stop him quickly.

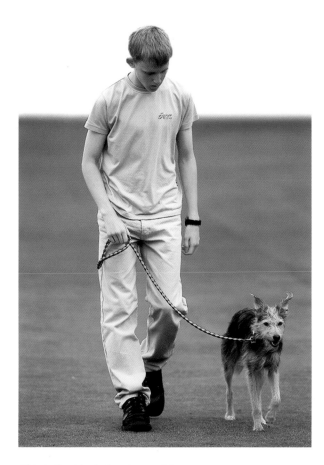

This is the ideal: the dog walking attentively and calmly at his owner's side. To achieve this, follow the steps on pages 60–61.

pages 60–61.

Don't forget

Always clean up after your dog if he defecates while on a walk. You can buy a special scoop and bags at a pet store, or simply carry a plastic bag in your pocket. Put the waste in a receptacle designed for the purpose (if available), double-bag it and place in a municipal trash can, or take it home and dispose of it there.

How to fit a headcollar

The correct use of a headcollar will prove invaluable when training your dog to walk with you. It allows you to apply gentle pressure on the leash that will turn the dog's head away from possible distractions.

This headcollar is too small for the dog: It's too high on the nose and close to the eyes.

This headcollar fits correctly.

To fit a headcollar, slip the nose band over the dog's nose as shown.

Position the headpiece around the back of the dog's head, gently lifting his ears out of the way.

Finally, fasten the headcollar.

Walking to heel

1 Begin with the dog on your left side, with his shoulder against your left leg and the leash held in your right hand as shown. Say your dog's name to get his attention, then "heel."

2 Begin walking purposefully.

3 If the dog walks in front of you or pulls, stop. He will no doubt look back at you in surprise.

Training to heel

At first, use the command "heel" only when your dog is in the required heel position, with his right shoulder next to your left leg, so he learns the word by association. Reinforce the command with a reward (praise or a treat) so the dog learns that this position is a pleasant one. Once he has learned where "heel" is, you can use the command to return him to that position.

Keeping up the pace

If your dog regularly lags behind, it could be because:

• You are walking too fast for him to keep up.

• He's more interested in sniffing to identify who else has been along that way previously, and possibly in marking his own passage.

4 Guide him back into position and get his attention as in step 1. Begin walking again. Patiently repeat as required, and your pet will soon get the idea.

In the first case, slow down a little. Dogs who are short-legged or old and stiff may find it difficult to maintain a brisk pace.

In the second case, you must be firmer with your dog and not allow him to "train" you to stop whenever he feels like it. Use a treat or toy to keep his attention on you and encourage him to keep up, or simply insist that he remain at heel.

☑ Key points

- Always remain alert when walking your dog so you are prepared for situations such as your dog suddenly jumping up at passersby or trying to run after another animal.

- Don't be lazy: Be sure you keep your dog at heel on all walks to reinforce his training.

- Some dogs do better on walks if they wear a headcollar rather than just a neck collar.

- Keep treats or a toy in your pocket; your dog is likely to stay at heel just in case a reward comes his way.

"Follow my pack leader"

Another method of keeping your dog's attention on you is by reinforcing your control. In order to do this, play "follow my pack leader."

1 Walk along as usual, with the dog by your left side.

2 Suddenly swing your left leg around and in front of the dog.

3 After swinging your leg round, change direction by turning fairly sharply.

4 Reward the dog with a treat or verbal praise. Repeat intermittently to keep him alert and reinforce your position as pack leader.

Sit

Having your dog in the sit position is the starting point for further essential training, such as lie down and stay. Four principles apply to training your dog to sit on command, and they may also be applied to heel training. The acronym ACER will help you remember them.

1 Attention
2 Command
3 Execute
4 Reward

Treat training

If you wish to use treats to train your dog to sit, follow these steps:

1 Stand beside your dog with the leash in your left hand, the dog on your right side, and a treat in your right hand.

2 Offer the treat, then give the command "sit" and at the same time move the treat up toward the dog's nose and over his head.

3 Move the treat back slightly so the dog is looking up.

4 He will automatically move into the sit position.

5 As he does, reward him with the treat.

Teaching him to sit

1 Stand with your dog on your left side, with the leash and a treat in your right hand, and get his **attention** by saying his name.

2 Command "sit" and simultaneously apply gentle pressure with your left hand on the dog's rear end to push him down.

3 Responding to the pressure, the dog will **execute** the command by sitting.

4 When he does, **reward** him with the treat.

✓ Key points

- Be patient when teaching the sit: Dogs feel vulnerable in this position, and depending on your dog's history, he may not be very comfortable with it.

- When you are out walking and want your dog to sit, slow down, then put him in the sit position.

- Practice the sit on walks to reinforce the command as well as your control.

- Always request that your dog sit before feeding him or putting on his leash.

- When rewarding with a treat, don't hold it so high that your dog jumps to get it.

- Remember: ACER!

Using a clicker

A clicker is a small handheld tool that can be used to "condition" good behavior. It's simple but effective: Just press and click.

The great thing about the clicker is that it is instant: The moment the dog displays a desired behavior, click, then reward with a tasty treat. The dog learns that the sound means a particular behavior is required, and this is reinforced by the reward that follows. Click, reward; no click, no reward. Being clever, dogs soon get the idea. You can also use a clicker when training a puppy.

Another good thing about a clicker is that you can use it at a distance, and the dog will come to you for his expected reward.

1 Stand with your dog and wait until he sits.

2 As soon as he does, click and say "sit" and/or use a hand signal.

3 Reward him with a treat and praise.

Lie down

Once your dog has learned to sit, as explained on pages 62–63, the next step is to teach him to lie down on command, then roll onto his side (see Roll Over on the opposite page).

Being able to have your dog do this, then let you handle him all over, is extremely handy for grooming and visits to the vet. You can also use the down position when you just want him to lie quietly while you are occupied with something else.

TRAINER'S TIP

• To teach your dog to sit up and then stand from a lying position, put a treat under his nose and raise it above his head, simultaneously saying "sit" or "stand." Reward him for the desired response with the treat.

• Practice each exercise separately at first and reward after each element. Then request a sit, down, and stay, and follow with a reward. Finally, request all of these and a stand after the stay, then give a reward. This usually turns out to be a game that the dog really enjoys.

Training him to lie down

1 With your dog in the sit position, get him to focus his attention on a treat in your hand.

2 Put the treat under his nose, then slowly move it down toward the floor or between his front paws. He will sink to the floor in his effort to get the treat. As soon as he does, say "down" and reward with the treat and praise. Practice this a couple of times, and you'll find that your dog soon learns to lie down on command in anticipation of a reward.

3 If all goes well, try extending the down into a stay. As you step away from the dog, say "stay" (with a hand signal as shown, if necessary), wait a couple of seconds, then go back to the dog and praise him lavishly. Gradually extend the distance between you and your dog as you command the stay. You'll be surprised at how quickly he learns to do this, too.

☑ Key points

- Instant reward is essential to teach these exercises effectively, because a dog is at his most vulnerable in a lying position. A reward will take his mind off that feeling and teach him that lying on command is pleasant and nonthreatening.

- Be patient. If you get annoyed, the dog will sense it, and you're unlikely to achieve your goal. Some dogs take longer than others to feel at ease with these exercises.

- Always finish the exercise on a positive note. If the dog gets bored, stop and ask him to do something he knows and enjoys, then reward so the lesson ends well. You can always try again tomorrow.

Roll over

With your dog in the down position, you can move on to the roll-over exercise. Because exposing his belly makes him feel vulnerable to potential attackers, your dog will lie on his side or back only if he feels safe and secure. You must teach this exercise carefully if you are to be successful and avoid stressing your dog. Attempt it only when both of you are relaxed and at ease with each other.

1 Show your dog a treat.

2 Move the treat closer to the dog's nose, then move it slowly around toward his shoulder, over the back of his neck, and down.

3 The dog's head will follow your hand until he has to lie flat on his side to keep the treat in sight.

4 At this point, say "roll over," give your dog the treat, and stroke his belly. Practice until he learns that "roll over" is a rewarding command to follow.

Stay

Having your dog stay where you want him, both indoors and out, is very useful. For instance, you can use this command if you have visitors and you want the dog to remain in his bed out of the way, or if he needs to stay put for his own safety and that of others while on a walk.

☑ Key points

- Always stay close to your dog as you move around him at first so he knows you are still there.

- Don't forget that the dog will get bored very quickly if you continue to practice the same thing over and over. If you get a positive result on the first attempt, don't repeat it. Finish on that good note.

- To release the dog from the stay, say the dog's name and then "here," adopting a welcoming posture to encourage him to come to you. Reward him when he does so.

- Dogs read body language well and will notice if you are bored with the training session, so stay alert and maintain the dog's attention.

Teaching him to stay

1 Put the dog into the sit position (see pages 62–63) by your left heel.

2 Command "stay," with the leash slack in your left hand. Hold your right hand with the palm open in front of your dog as a visual signal. Repeat the "stay" command as you take a step out to the side of the dog.

TRAINER'S TIP

Stay can be difficult for an adopted dog to learn because he may feel that he is being abandoned. The best advice is to be patient and stay close to him until he realizes that you aren't leaving him.

3 Repeat the command, then walk briskly around the dog, staying close to him so he knows where you are.

4 When you complete the circuit, you should be standing by your dog's right side. Reward with praise and a treat if desired. Repeat the exercise, this time moving a little farther away at the front but coming close again at the back to reassure the dog that you are still there.

5 You will be able to further develop the stay as the dog becomes more confident that you are not abandoning him and is comfortable with staying put. Extend the leash and increase the distance as you walk in front of the dog and around him.

Free stay

Once your dog is happy to stay put, you can progress to the free stay. Move away from him, command "stay," and drop the leash (if you want, you can put one foot on the leash at first). Wait a few seconds, then walk back to and around the dog, finishing by his right side. Reward him with praise and a treat.

Away

This command is very useful for sending your dog to his bed or crate or away from something you don't want him near. The method of teaching it is simple but extremely effective.

By giving your dog one of his favorite treats, showing him that there are more to be had, and placing the treat container in his view, you will ensure that he won't want to move from his position. He will naturally feel the need to keep the treats in sight, in the hope of receiving another one.

Using treats to teach "away"

1 Slice some really tasty treats, such as hot dogs, into small pieces. Put them in a plastic container with a lid and show them to your dog.

The command "away" can be used to send a dog out of the room.

TRAINER'S TIP

Always finish on a positive note so the dog remembers a pleasant experience with the "away" command.

2 Using the "away" command, guide the dog to his bed (or out of the room), reward him, and place the container of treats next to him so he can see them.

3 Because the treats are so close, the dog will be reluctant to leave his position. Reinforce this with a "stay" command and reward him again. In this way, he'll come to regard wherever he is as a nice place to be.

4 Continue with whatever it is that you want to do while your dog is away from you. If he comes to you without being called, simply repeat the exercise, using "away" as you put him back in his bed or out of the room.

☑ Key points

- Keep the exercise short to start with, so your dog doesn't become bored and switch off.

- Ignore your dog if he comes back to you uninvited, then return him to the position in which you left him, again using the "away" command.

- At first, don't wait too long before calling the dog back to you, or he'll get bored and come looking for you.

- Practice this exercise often so your dog learns by reward association that "away" is a good command to obey.

Street safety

Knowing how to cross a street correctly with your dog is vital for everyone's safety. He should cross *with* you, not be dragged across by you or vice versa. There is obvious danger in an owner struggling across a street with a dog who is out of control.

In order to be able to cross safely, your dog must obey the "sit" command. (If you need to review this, see pages 62–63.) Only when your dog is sitting calmly and quietly by your side can you concentrate fully on the traffic to be sure the street is absolutely clear before you cross. An ill-trained dog is a danger not only to himself and you but also to drivers and other pedestrians.

TRAINER'S TIP

Using a retractable leash isn't a good idea when walking your dog near traffic. If he should dash out into the path of vehicles, you may not be able to stop him quickly enough.

Crossing safely

1 If your dog is not used to traffic, accustom him to the sights and sounds by taking him to a spot where you can sit and watch traffic go by without being too close. Distract him by offering small pieces of food or a desirable toy. Don't fuss over him or hold him; that will just make him feel that there is something to be afraid of. Speak to him in a normal tone.

2 Once the dog appears unbothered by the traffic, walk him quietly on the sidewalk, again distracting him as vehicles approach. Reward him after they have passed. Soon he will look to you for a reward and ignore the traffic.

☑ **Key points**

- Start by training on quiet streets.

- Be sure that your dog's collar is adjusted correctly so he can't slip out of it and escape into the street.

- Leash length is important. It must be a suitable type for the size of your dog and not too long for good handling and control.

- Keep your dog in the sit position as traffic is passing so he is under control until you're ready to cross.

- Be sure you have the dog's attention before stepping off the curb.

3 When crossing the street, stop at a point where you have a good view in both directions. Avoid crossing at intersections unless there is a pedestrian crossing. Command your dog to sit at the heel position while you check whether the street is safe to cross. Continue to remind the dog to stay, keeping his attention on you with a treat, toy, or verbal encouragement until you cross.

4 Cross only when the street is clear in both directions. Keep checking for approaching vehicles and keep your dog's attention on you by holding a treat in the hand closest to him.

Retrieve

Throwing a toy for your dog to retrieve is a good way to see that he gets adequate exercise. It's also a game that both of you can enjoy, at least for as long as your arm holds out. But if a dog won't retrieve for you, how do you get him interested in playing "fetch" in the first place?

High-value toys

First, you need to use a toy that you can take from the dog's mouth easily, without endangering your fingers. Try a Kong on a rope, a ball on a rope, a suitably sized rubber ring, or a rubber tug toy. These are all "high-value" toys because of their throw/chase/tug-of-war attributes.

It's important to let your dog play with a high-value toy only when you have control of it. Play with your dog, then put the toy away when the game or training session is finished so the toy retains its special status for the dog.

A rope toy, rubber ring, and rubber tug toy.

Teaching him to retrieve

1 First use an everyday (low-value) toy as the item to be retrieved, but have the high-value toy in your pocket or hidden behind your back to use as the reward once your dog brings the everyday toy back to you. Have the dog at heel in a sit-stay position (see pages 63–64 and 66–67 to review these exercises), then throw the low-value toy, saying "fetch" at the same time.

2 Once the dog has the toy, call him back to you by saying his name and "fetch."

TRAINER'S TIP

If you let your dog spit out the toy or drop it at your feet, it may be a problem if you ever want to take part in fun obedience competitions with him. Right from the start, train him to "give" by releasing the toy into your hand.

3 When he comes to you, reward him with praise or a treat and the high-value toy. Repeat once or twice, and finish on a positive note.

4 If your dog will chase the toy but not bring it to you, show him the high-value toy to entice him. Most dogs cannot resist this.

5 Praise the dog lavishly when he returns with the low-value toy, then play a game with the high-value toy. Your dog will soon get the message: No low-value toy, no game.

6 Another ploy you can try when the dog won't bring his toy back to you is to walk away from him. Thinking he is being left, he will usually trot after you. When he does, drop down on one knee and call him, then give a treat when he comes. If that fails, simply turn your back on the dog; he'll wonder why you are ignoring him and will come to you seeking reassurance. Reward him when he does.

(continued)

7 Once the dog has gotten the hang of fetching the low-value toy, clip on a long training leash, toss the high-value toy out a yard or two, and say "fetch." The dog will almost certainly dash out and pick it up.

8 Next, you want the dog to bring the toy back to you, at which point you can give him a reward. As he picks up the toy, call "fetch" again. He should then return to you. If he doesn't, use the leash to coax him gently.

9 As the dog approaches you, take hold of the toy and start a gentle tug game, letting the dog win as his reward for bringing you the toy. Repeat the exercise, but this time, you win the toy by taking it from him. Say "leave" and put the toy away. This will end the exercise on a positive note and leave the dog wanting that toy, so he'll be eager to play the game next time. After this, play with that particular toy only when you have time to play fetch.

Tug of war

Introduce the toy to the dog by offering it to him; if he takes hold of his end, have a gentle tug of war. Initially, keep the tug games short so the dog doesn't get bored; stop the game with him still wanting to continue, so the next time you play, he will be eager to join in.

After a short game, take the toy from the dog, giving a "leave" command; reward him with a treat and/or praise when he releases (gives) it. You can stop using food treats once he gets the hang of what he is supposed to do, since the expectation of the next play session will be reward enough in itself.

Fetch

Now that the dog is interested in the toy, you can train him to bring an item back to you.

Give

Once your dog has learned to fetch, the next step is to teach him to release the toy into your hand. To control the situation and the distance the dog can travel, put him on a leash for this exercise.

☑ Key points

- Make the games short and pleasant. Your dog will quickly lose interest in a toy if the game is boring.

- Alternate winners when you play tug games, or the dog won't want to play when he realizes that he will never win the prize.

- When playing tug games with your dog, move the toy sideways, not up and down, to avoid damaging his neck or spine.

- Never force your dog to release an item by shouting at him, smacking him, or grabbing and pulling at the "prize." This may make him aggressive and possessive of his toys because it reinforces the notion that the item is important and should be jealously guarded.

- Don't expect the dog to understand the exercise immediately. He's used to playing with his toys, not retrieving them and giving them to you.

Let go!

If your dog won't let go of the toy, here's how you can make him release it.

1 Be calm and quiet but determined.

2 Using the leash, coax the dog to you. Then ask him to sit; it's always easier to deal with a dog who is sitting rather than jumping around.

3 Take hold of the toy but don't pull it; place the thumb and forefinger of your free hand under the dog's muzzle. Apply gentle pressure to his jowls, pushing them up and over his bottom teeth. At the same time, give the command "give." The dog will then release his grip, and you'll be able to take the toy. The intention, of course, is not to hurt the dog but just to make him a bit uncomfortable until he releases the toy.

After repeating this exercise two or three times, you'll find that as soon as you put your finger and thumb under the dog's jaw, he will respond to your command. In the future, you'll be able to call the dog into the sit position in front of you, reach for the toy and say "give," and the dog will release it into your hand.

Recall

Once your dog knows his name, you need to train him to come back to you (recall) the instant you call him. This is essential for safety when he is off-leash and running free.

If the dog knows that coming back to you means he will be rewarded, he is more likely to do so. Initially, the reward should be of high value, such as a really tasty treat or a prized toy, but as your dog becomes conditioned to return to you on command, praise will probably be sufficient. You can, however, give occasional high-value rewards to maintain immediate response.

Testing time

When your dog is obediently coming back to you the first time you call, try the recall exercise with one or two calm dogs you both know, first on a long leash for control and in case you need to reinforce the exercise from the beginning.

Approach the other (leashed) dogs with your dog on an extended leash. Before they meet and greet, call him back to you by saying his name and then "come" or "here." If your dog comes to you, praise him lavishly and give him a treat or toy. If not, simply reel the leash in and drop to one knee as he nears, encouraging him to come to you and rewarding him as he reaches you. Then try again.

Once your dog is recalling well in this situation, try him off-leash, but go back to using the leash if you are unsuccessful. Work toward doing the exercise with all the dogs off-leash.

Teaching him to come to you

1 To begin, walk forward with your dog on a long leash and at heel as usual. Then allow the leash to go slack and move backward, calling your dog's name and the command "come" at the same time. Offer a treat or high-value toy to elicit a quick response.

Stop!

This exercise, which is similar to the recall, is used if you need to stop the dog suddenly when he's walking on the leash—for example, if you have just seen some broken glass hidden in the grass directly in front of him, you need him to stop instantly to keep him from stepping on it. You can use either the "stop" or "stay" command, but be consistent.

To begin, walk along at a normal pace with the leash in your left hand, shortened so there's not much slack, and the dog at heel. Then slow down a little to give yourself time to do the following: Simultaneously say the command "stop," give a quick tug backward on the leash, and bring your right hand down, palm open, in a sharp chopping motion in front of the dog.

Practice speeding up this command, and reward your dog each time he responds instantly. The idea is to eliminate the need to stop the dog physically with the leash and to have him respond to your voice and hand signal alone.

2 As the dog reaches you, say "sit," and when he responds, give the treat or play a game with the toy and praise him lavishly. Once the dog is responding instantly each time you do this exercise, try dropping the leash on the ground (within easy reach in case you need to grab it) to see what his reaction is. When you are happy with the dog's response, try the exercise off-leash in a secure area, gradually increasing the distance between you.

TRAINER'S **TIP**

Take this exercise slowly: You don't want to move too fast, too soon and have to keep going back to the beginning. Eventually, this will have a negative effect, and your dog will start to ignore your recall command.

Sit-stay

The natural progression from the stop-stay exercise is to a sit-stay, first with the dog on a long leash, then off-leash.

To begin, have the dog ahead of you on the long leash. Call his name to get his attention, then step toward him (rather than have him come back to you) with your hand up, palm facing the dog, and command "sit-stay." When he does, walk up to him and give him a reward. Then try it again, but this time call the dog to you after the sit-stay, and reward him on his return.

Alternate walking to and calling the dog so he doesn't become accustomed to the same exercise but will stop, sit, and stay on command both on and off the leash, waiting for you either to go up to him or command him to come to you.

Off-leash emergency stop

Occasionally, when you are out on a walk with your dog off-leash, you may encounter a situation where you suddenly need to stop your dog in his tracks and have him return to you. You can effect such an emergency stop by using either a shake can or a dog training whistle.

☑ Key points

- Be sure to train the recall and stop exercises in a safe, enclosed area—not a local park.

- Your dog must recall on command before you move on to the stop exercise.

- If problems arise, go back a couple of steps and reinforce these before going on. If you still have difficulty, consult a trainer. It's very important that your dog recalls or stops when you want him to.

- Practice the recall and stop regularly, but in short sessions.

- Always finish on a success. If the dog recalls or stops the first time, end the lesson there, leaving him with a positive association.

Emergency stop

1 Use a shake can—a metal or plastic container half-filled with small pebbles that make a loud noise when shaken. Shake the can to catch the dog's attention and stop him in his tracks. Immediately call his name and offer an irresistible treat.

2 Instead of a shake can, you can use a dog training whistle. Keep it on a chain around your neck when you are out with your dog so you have immediate access to it if necessary.

3 If the dog runs after something, give a sharp blast on the whistle. This should make him stop and look back to see where the sudden noise has come from.

4 The instant your dog looks back, call him to you and reward him with a treat when he returns.

Socialization

If your dog is well socialized with humans and other animals, he is less likely to develop behavior problems. Dogs generally love being with humans and their own kind, so it's important to socialize your dog so both of you can enjoy the company of others without stress. The principles of socializing puppies also apply to adult dogs (see pages 42–43).

If you have an adult dog who hasn't been socialized properly—that is, he has not had the chance to meet many people or other dogs—you need to address this situation carefully and correctly. The best way to do this is to find a good training school that holds socialization classes for older dogs in a safe environment. Doing this will make you feel more confident, especially if your dog gets overexcited or even becomes aggressive when he meets people or other dogs and you're not sure how to cope with the situation.

Introductions

Having a dog who will sit and stay on command (see pages 62–63 and 66–67) is the key to successful introduction and interaction. If you can control your dog calmly, you stand a better chance of having him accept the situations around him so that interacting with other people and animals is pleasant for both of you.

The ideal is to have a dog that you know is there, but who doesn't let you know he's there. Teaching your dog to sit quietly when visitors call makes life more pleasant for all concerned.

When starting to socialize your dog, remember that you can't force him to accept friends; he has to do it at his own pace. What you can do is help him simply by staying calm yourself. If he feels the leash begin to tighten, he will get the impression that you aren't happy with the situation, and he'll react in kind. Try to let the leash stay a little bit slack, although not too loose. If you give him too much room to move about, he may panic.

☑ Key points

- Don't force your dog to socialize; give him time and the opportunity to accept others at his own pace. Forcing him may result in an aggressive or nervous dog.

- Avoid overenthusiastic offers of help and advice that may push the dog in the wrong direction.

- Don't be afraid to seek professional help from a trainer. Socialization is an important aspect of your dog's emotional makeup.

- Make visitors aware of your rules regarding the dog, such as not giving him attention the minute they walk in to avoid elevating his status and encouraging him to seek attention.

- For the safety of both parties, don't let children play with a dog unsupervised.

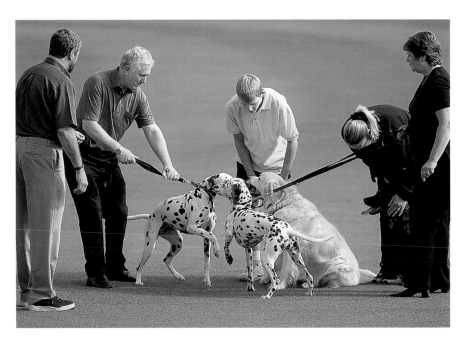

A dog who is willing to play is a happy dog. Taking your dog to classes where he can socialize with others will bring out the best in him.

It's important that children—and even adult visitors, for that matter—know not to take liberties with your dog, such as grabbing at his tail or paws in play or encouraging him to play-bite at arms or clothing.

Appropriate play

There is a tendency for children to rush straight up to any dog they see and put their hands all over him or even give him a hug. This is a potentially frightening experience for the dog, as he doesn't know that the child's intentions are nonthreatening. He may view the action as aggressive and snap to protect himself.

It's important to keep an eye on children when they are playing with a dog. They can get carried away and not realize when a game is getting out of hand, with the dog becoming overexcited and therefore liable to play rough.

Discourage children from playing tug games with your dog, because they may not know when to stop. The dog could become reluctant to relinquish the tug and become aggressive toward the child.

Human hands

If you have a chance to meet people you know in the park, it's fine, but don't try to push your dog into meeting others. Don't let your friends approach the dog and reach straight down to touch him; instead, ask them to ignore him initially and perhaps drop a treat or two in front of him. You will be surprised at how quickly he'll want to investigate a hand that's dropping treats!

The point of this exercise is that the dog approaches the hand and not the other way around, so he sees hands as nonthreatening. The reason for this tactic is this: You may not know the history of the dog, especially if he is from an animal shelter. If he was physically abused in the past, he may well be hand-shy and either duck away from an approaching hand or snap at it as a defensive measure.

House manners

It's important for your dog to understand his place in the household and behave appropriately. For example, you should be able to greet visitors at the door without your dog rushing to get there first or refusing to let them in. It's not his job to greet them; it's your place as pack leader to do that.

If your dog doesn't understand this, you may find that after a while, people will stop visiting, and you may even start to lose friends. If this is the case, your dog is doing you no favors; likewise, by not training him to socialize properly, you are being unfair to him.

Take the lead

There are certain things you can do to put into practice house rules that your dog understands. When you come home, do what you need to do first, such as putting the groceries away. Do anything at all *except* go straight to the dog and give him attention.

While the dog is rushing around demanding attention, ignore him. You don't want to reinforce his notion that he has high status in the household and should be your top priority. After two or three minutes, he will become bored with being ignored and will either find something to do or lie down. At this point, call him and give him a few minutes of attention.

Explain this strategy to your guests, and if they agree to go along with it, let the dog be in the same room. Ask your friends to sit down and ignore the dog. If he tries to get up on a guest's lap or chair, have your friend gently but firmly push him down without saying anything to him. Even a reprimand would fulfill his desire for attention. After a few minutes, he will go away.

Leave him for a short time and then call him to you, using his name and the command "come." Give him attention for a little while, then gently push him away with the command "finish," and remove your arms and hands from his reach.

By introducing these few firm rules, you'll soon see a change in the dog's behavior. He will not always demand your attention or be under your feet. When in the house, you have the right to sit and read, relax, or work: It's simply bad manners for the dog to put himself in your way or pester you.

TRAINER'S TIP

Remember to be consistent with house rules so the dog doesn't become confused; not allowing him to do something one day and then allowing it the next may result in stress- or anxiety-induced behaviors.

Enforce house rules

Here is a typical example of a dog with no house manners: You need to go from one room to another, but as you get up, the dog also gets up and stands or lies in the doorway, blocking your exit. You end up either trying to move him out of the way or stepping over him. This is a mistake, as you're giving control of the situation to the dog and thereby elevating his status. So how do you get your dog to understand what you want? Remember, if he doesn't understand, he can't possibly do as you wish.

With a dog who insists on sitting or standing in the doorway as you are trying to pass through, you should first try to preempt the behavior and deal with it before it becomes a problem. As you are getting up from your seat, give the dog a "stay" command, which tells him what you want him to do. Provided you have taught the dog what this means, he should obey. If you haven't taught him to stay, he won't be able to comply. (Teaching a dog to stay is described on pages 66–67.)

If your dog is already standing or lying in the doorway, tell him to move using the "away" command; do *not* step over him. (Teaching away is described on pages 68–69.)

As you try to exit the room, you find your dog lying in front of the doorway.

Use the "away" command rather than simply stepping over him.

How to stop attention-seeking behavior

GOLDEN RULES

Remember these three rules:

• You pay the bills, therefore you are the pack leader.

• Your dog is just that—a dog. He does not contribute to providing food, warmth, and shelter for the pack.

• This means that you are number one in the pecking order, and your dog is at the bottom.

1 If your dog demands your attention by jumping up and pawing at your legs while you are doing something else, such as trying to read, you should ignore him.

2 When he gets no reaction from you, he will sit down and consider the situation.

3 The dog will lie down quietly while deciding what his next move should be.

4 Soon after he lies down, it's important that you reward this desired behavior. This way, the dog will associate non-attention-seeking behavior with a pleasant, positive experience and learn that leaping around trying to get attention brings no reward at all.

☑ **Key points**

- Your dog is a dog, not a human member of the family.

- If you treat your dog as a human, he will treat you as a dog.

- If you give in to the dog in the first instance, you are paving the way for a lot of other undesirable behavior traits to develop.

- The dog needs to know where he fits into the family group; you both need to know that his position is at the bottom of the ladder.

- A settled dog will be a happier dog, while a spoiled dog will not enjoy life to its fullest.

Reinforce the pack hierarchy

When you are teaching your dog manners, setting rules for feeding is essential. In the wild, a pack of dogs has a leader who provides food; the leader also eats first. You should imitate this behavior by making it clear that the family eats before the dog is allowed his food. Try the following exercise.

1 Place the dog's food bowl on the table while you prepare his meal. Make him sit quietly while you do this.

2 Place a plate of cookies behind the bowl.

3 Get each family member to take a cookie and eat it while the dog watches; it will appear to him that you are eating from his bowl.

4 After you have done this, leave the dog for a few minutes, then come back and put his food on the floor, saying "leave" as you do. Wait until the dog looks at you for permission, then let him eat.

Through this exercise, the order of the pack hierarchy is reinforced: The human family members head the list, with the dog at the bottom.

CORRECTIVE TRAINING:
The most common problems

Training Plan

Week 1

- To combat separation anxiety, gradually reduce the dog's dependence on you and implement an appropriate socialization program (see pages 80–81).

- Restrict him to certain areas of the house that are easy to clean in case of soiling. Begin housebreaking. Implement a feeding routine that includes going outside shortly after eating.

- Don't leave him for prolonged periods where he is unable to relieve himself.

- Provide activity toys to occupy him when he is left alone.

- Restrict access to furniture that the dog likes to sit on and begin "climbing on furniture" training (see pages 114–115).

- Begin training to prevent pulling on the leash (see pages 100–101).

- Go back to basics with house manners (see pages 82–85) and food training (see pages 52–53) to reinforce his status within the family "pack."

Week 2

- After a week of the corrective training outlined for week 1, you should see a difference in all problem areas. Continue with training as necessary.

- If you haven't already done so, use a command for urinating and defecating.

Week 3

By now, provided you have implemented a care and training routine that works for you and your dog, it's likely that you have resolved all problems or are three-quarters of the way toward doing so.

Week 4

If you're not starting to see a change in behavior (or if it's actually getting worse), it's probably time to get professional help. Your vet may be able to recommend a reputable trainer.

"Why does my dog misbehave?" is a question that dog trainers hear all the time. But think about it: Is your dog really misbehaving, or is he doing what *he* thinks is the right thing?

There are a number of reasons why dogs behave as they do. Usually, it's because they have been forced into it by human interference. In a wild pack, dogs interact naturally with one another and with other animals. They quickly learn the pecking order and social skills within the pack, as well as exactly where they fit into it.

How long does corrective training take?

You have a good chance of solving a problem behavior in just a few days by following up two days of intensive training with continual reinforcement. This is needed to stay on top of the problem and gradually refocus the dog on what type of behavior is and isn't rewarding for him.

If your dog has two or more habits that you would like to change, you can work on them simultaneously. To work out a training program, assess your dog's needs and read the detailed instructions on areas of corrective training in the following pages. Then break down your training needs into progressive sections.

The chart at left is a sample training schedule for a fit, healthy dog who pulls on the leash, jumps on furniture, and soils in the house.

Depending on how the training progresses from week to week, along with the amount of time you can devote to caring for your dog, you may achieve your goal of a leash-obedient, housebroken, and mannerly dog in less time than suggested here. On the other hand, it could take longer.

The first step is to ascertain why the dog is behaving this way. He could have a physical problem, so he must first be checked by a vet. Did something happen that triggered the behavior? Keep a diary of when the problems occur. Provided that the vet gives the dog a clean bill of health, reasons for his behavior may include:

• Separation anxiety. Some dogs display such behaviors when left on their own.
• A lack of basic training.
• A lack of basic care; for example, the dog has no access to an outside place to relieve himself. Or he may not be getting enough exercise and is so keen to go for walks that he pulls on the leash.

The human factor

With domesticated dogs, it's the human element that upsets the natural status quo. A dog enters a household as a puppy quite willing to learn from the pack leaders, but in many cases, the human pack leader who should be setting the examples and rules throws them straight out the window because "the dog looked at me with those lovely brown eyes."

As soon as you give in to the first whim of your puppy or adult dog, you're on the way to having a pet who, from your perspective, misbehaves. The dog sees this as his chance to become the leader of the pack in his own environment.

TRAINER'S TIP

There is often no quick-fix solution for some types of behavior problems, such as aggression, chasing other animals, and car travel problems, so you have to be prepared for a prolonged, sustained program of retraining.

Guilt trip

Human beings believe that because they look and feel guilty about doing something wrong, so does a dog. However, this is not necessarily the way a dog sees things. A prime example is a dog who has soiled in the house. Since this behavior is a natural function, why should he feel guilty?

The dog's timid appearance when you come home to the dirty floor is probably not due to his guilt at having soiled but to your angry tone of voice and hostile body language. Instead of being annoyed with the dog, you should be cross with yourself.

Aim to solve the "problem" by asking yourself how it could have been prevented.

How old is the dog? Could he reasonably be expected to last the length of time you were gone without needing to relieve himself? More important, ask yourself if you have housebroken your dog correctly so that he knows where to go. (For details on housebreaking and dealing with soiling in the house, see pages 46–47 and 102–103.)

The following pages demonstrate how you can correct problems that have developed or have come with a dog you've adopted. The key to all successful corrective training is not to show anger at the dog, which won't achieve anything positive; instead, show him an alternative that is more rewarding for everyone. And you can make huge progress in just minutes a day!

TRAINER'S TIP

A dog who guards his food or toys is a liability. Sooner or later, someone is likely to be bitten. Teaching your dog not to be possessive is essential right from the start (see pages 72–75).

How owners cause problems

Attention-seeking

A dog playing tug with his owner will quickly realize he is the boss if allowed to win all the time. He should not be allowed to dictate when to play, either. Instead, you should begin the game by inviting him to play. Then he must recognize when the game is over, which is when you have had enough. All too often, the dog continues to toss the toy onto his owner's knee, and instead of ignoring him, the owner throws the toy on the floor just for a bit of peace. The dog immediately realizes that he has his owner's attention, and the game will continue on his terms.

Chewing

If you give your puppy or adult dog an old shoe or item of clothing to play with, don't be surprised if you find him taking and chewing the family's clothes and shoes. After all, he can't differentiate between the items you no longer need and the ones you do!

Sitting on furniture

A dog doesn't just decide that he is going to sit on the furniture. Probably at some point, he was invited up onto his owner's knee because "he was cute and wanted to cuddle." In the wild, these animals obviously wouldn't have furniture to sit on, so it's the owner who causes the problem in the first place.

Rough play

If you decide to get down on the floor and play-wrestle with the dog, it's likely that he will try to dominate the situation: He'll end up on top, and you'll be lying on the floor with the dog chewing on various parts of your body. This is the point at which you will start to get up and tell the dog to leave you alone because he has probably nipped you, and it hurts! You think your dog has become badly behaved or too aggressive, but actually he is only doing exactly what he would do in a pack situation. You may tolerate this behavior in a puppy, but it can become a real problem in an adult dog.

Begging and stealing

If you make the mistake of feeding your dog scraps from the table because he looks hungry or he was in an animal shelter and you feel you have to make up for the poor start he had in life, you're creating a big problem for yourself. The dog will start helping himself from the table or counter, and he will sit and salivate while you're preparing or eating your meal. He'll start to beg for food, and if that doesn't work, he'll sit and bark until you give him food from your plate.

From a dog's point of view

The human misunderstanding of the role of the pack leader leads to behavior problems. At the risk of indulging in anthropomorphism (see page 15), let's take a look at this from the dog's point of view.

"Hey, I've got a new owner. I wonder if he's going to be like the last one. It seems like they all want us to do things for them, but I don't know what it means when I'm off the leash in the park and my owner starts to chase me around, shouting and screaming. What does 'come here' mean, anyway? Whenever my old owner shouted 'come here' and caught me, he gave me a beating. Well, if this one thinks I'll fall for that again, he has another think coming.

"These people are funny creatures. They get you home and give you a smelly old slipper to play with, then when you've chewed that up and find a fresh one, they get really angry. It's only a slipper, after all, just like the one they gave you in the first place.

"They let you get up on the sofa when you're a puppy, and then later, when you weigh more and slobber all over the place, they don't like it. And another thing: Why is it all right to sit on your favorite chair until company comes, but then you're expected to give it up for one of them?

"I wish that people who take us in would decide what they want from us in the first place, then explain what they mean when they say something. After all, I am a dog—a pet—and I'm just here to please. If only I knew how."

Aggressive behavior

Aggression in dogs is not always what it seems: Sometimes, what a human perceives as a bad temper or nastiness is actually fear. The dog is being defensive because he has learned that showing his teeth and growling usually cause potential adversaries—or anyone causing him discomfort—to back off. Whatever the reason, it presents a problem for owners.

Aggressive behavior is extremely difficult to overcome unless you're prepared to invest time and money in retraining. Sadly, sometimes aggression is so deeply ingrained and the dog so unpredictable that there is no option other than euthanasia. However, these cases are rare, and with the right approach and commitment from the owner, it's possible to turn an outwardly aggressive, bad-tempered dog into a more affable and even-tempered companion.

Teaching nonaggressive behavior

1 An owner can unwittingly cause a dog to become aggressive toward other dogs or people. For instance, when you're out walking and your dog tries to hide behind you when another person or dog approaches, the worst thing you can do is try to reassure him. He'll decide that if he needs reassurance, there really must be something to be afraid of. Sensing your tension, he will snap as a defensive measure. If this works (it usually does) and the "adversary" backs off, your dog learns that his behavior achieves the desired result. Sadly, you then perceive the dog as being aggressive.

2 Instead of reacting to your dog's nervousness, simply ignore him and continue what you're doing. This in itself will reassure your dog that there is nothing to be frightened of and he has no need to be defensive.

TRAINER'S **TIP**

Professional help is a must when dealing with aggression in any form. Find a good trainer who can help and advise you on the most appropriate retraining for your dog. Trainers see this kind of behavior all the time and know the best ways to deal with it, while also taking into account the owner's capabilities and lifestyle.

3 To begin, retrain your dog in situations with people and dogs whom you know so the other owners fully understand what you're trying to do and will respect the need for a controlled "meet and greet" session with their dogs. Let your dog investigate the other dog or person in his own time; don't force an introduction. Once he reassures himself that there is no need to take defensive action, he'll relax. Then you can praise him and give him a treat. This way, he learns to view other people or dogs as rewarding rather than as potential threats.

(continued)

When a dog barks and appears aggressive toward passersby while out walking, and the owner is unable to get the dog's attention despite his best efforts, it shows that the owner has very little control. If this sounds familiar, you might try using a headcollar on your dog. Not only will this give him something to think about other than terrorizing passersby, it will also give you more control. But talk to a trainer about it first, since some items of equipment may actually make the situation worse, depending on the reason for your dog's aggression.

4 Taking your dog to socialization classes is extremely beneficial. At first, it will be an on-leash experience with other well-trained and nonaggressive dogs of a similar size (a small dog would be even more intimidated in a class of Great Danes!). Gradually, you can progress to mixing with all types of dogs off-leash as yours becomes more confident and therefore more sociable.

5 Agility classes are great for socialization. The dogs are usually too busy enjoying themselves to think of viewing their classmates as adversaries, and by the time the session is over, they have discovered that it's much more rewarding to play together than to fight.

Without a headcollar, your dog is easily able to look at a passerby and bark to his heart's content.

With a headcollar, you can gently turn your dog's head so he has to look away from the passerby.

Case history: Nervous aggression

THE DOG • While working with a class at an animal shelter, Keith Davis was approached by Rhonda and Jack. With them was a little dog with his tail curled between his legs and his ears folded down. He could not have tucked himself any tighter into the back of Rhonda's legs if he had tried. He was truly terrified. The dog, named Billy, was 4½ years old and had been adopted from a shelter.

THE PROBLEM • As Rhonda explained, Billy was aggressive to people who passed by or stopped to talk to them and also toward dogs that he saw— and if they dared to come near her, he went crazy. When Keith approached Billy, his response was a bark and a growl to show his full set of teeth.

THE SOLUTION • Keith told Rhonda and Jack to take Billy away from everyone else and just to sit and watch the class at work. Keith then worked the class closer and closer to where the three were sitting. Introducing treats in order to distract Billy proved very helpful, and soon he was watching and listening to Rhonda, who spoke to him every time a dog or owner came near. When Billy responded to her voice, he was rewarded.

This initial work continued for a couple of sessions, then progressed to Rhonda and Billy walking around the training area but ignoring what everyone else was doing in class. The next step was to include Billy in the group for the socializing exercises and, with Rhonda using the same method of treat distraction, he soon began to ignore people and dogs who walked past at a distance. Gradually his classmates came closer and closer, until eventually another dog was able to sit next to Billy without any adverse reaction from him.

Over a period of time, Billy was allowed off-leash for short periods to check his response (the other dogs in the class were well-trained and kept on-leash). He was initially very reluctant to leave Rhonda, but over several weeks he gradually began to investigate the perimeter of the training area and was willing to approach a couple of the quieter dogs.

At this point, Keith encouraged other handlers to talk to but not touch Billy and to offer him treats, which he took. Suddenly he seemed much more confident in his surroundings. He would even allow Keith to stroke him, although only while he was standing with Rhonda and Jack.

While Billy would never be the most confident dog in the world, he was now quite happy to walk around without becoming a nervous wreck if someone looked at him. Rhonda was overjoyed; because of the training sessions, she could at least take Billy for a run in the park, and more important, she knew he was enjoying life a whole lot more.

When dogs bite

If the problem is so severe that your dog actually bites, or you're sure that it's only a matter of time until he does, it's essential to seek help from a professional trainer, especially if there are children in the house. You can't hope to deal effectively with the problem yourself.

In the meantime, don't walk your dog—and certainly don't let him off the leash in public places—without a muzzle. Actually, it's safer not to exercise him in public places at all, since with a muzzle on he would not be able to defend himself if another dog attacked him.

TRAINER'S TIP

At the very first indication of a problem with aggression in your dog, no matter how slight, seek advice from a trainer. With professional help, it's likely that you can prevent any serious problems from developing.

Fitting a muzzle

1 When using a muzzle, you must be sure it fits correctly, or your dog will be uncomfortable, which will only increase his aggression. If you're unsure about the best muzzle to use, ask a trainer. To put a muzzle on, first slip it gently over the dog's nose.

2 Put the headpiece behind the dog's head, carefully lifting his ears out of the way so they don't get trapped.

3 Fasten the headpiece, then check to be sure it isn't too tight by sliding the flat of your hand between it and the dog's neck. Conversely, if it isn't tight enough, the dog will be able to dislodge it easily.

✓ Key points

- With any form of aggression, seek immediate advice and practical help from an experienced trainer. Don't try dealing with the problem on your own; it won't work.

- Don't let your dog gain the upper hand at home. Pay particular attention to food training, socializing, and house manners (see pages 52–53 and 80–85).

- Take your dog for a veterinary examination to see if the aggression is due to an underlying physical problem that's causing discomfort and making him irritable.

- Your demeanor and actions toward your dog have a huge effect on his temperament. A stressed-out, irritable owner tends to pass on his tension to his dog, resulting in a nervous, defensive animal who is likely to develop into an aggressive one.

- The importance of socializing your dog can't be overemphasized: Attending training classes at least once a week will gradually make a difference in any but the most emotionally disabled dog.

Case history: Jealous aggression

THE DOG • Bob, a five-year-old golden retriever, belonged to Margaret and John. They got him as a pup, and he had spent all his time with John. But then it got to the point where Bob had taken over, deciding who could come into the house and what people could and couldn't do inside the home. He became aggressive toward visitors and began to threaten other family members.

THE PROBLEM • When the couple started to look after their three-year-old grandson, Bob became jealous of the attention given to the toddler and actually mouthed the child's body. Understandably, the little boy's parents refused to let him return to his grandparents' home until the dog had been either dealt with or destroyed.

THE SOLUTION • Keith Davis visited the home without the child being present, and as he walked in, he encountered warning signs of aggression from Bob. It was apparent to Keith that Bob had decided that he was now top dog and therefore in charge of the household. Keith advised the owners of a suitable retraining routine that would, over a period of time, reinstate them as pack leaders. This involved the couple ignoring Bob until he had settled down and not playing with him or fussing over him if he demanded attention. In addition, they were told to teach Bob to leave the room on command and to sit or lie quietly and stay where he was told until they called him to them.

Over a number of weeks, Margaret and John taught Bob that it was all right to bark when people knocked at the door, but then, on command, he had to go and lie down quietly and not greet visitors until requested to do so. Keith also advised Bob's owners to change their feeding routine so it placed the dog at the bottom of the pack by giving Bob his meal only after they had finished theirs.

Eventually, the grandchild was introduced back into the equation: The plan was to make Bob understand that the little boy was a higher-ranking pack member, not a lower one and therefore a threat to his perceived position as top dog. Under adult supervision, this was implemented by the child eating first, then giving Bob a treat so the dog viewed him as a source of pleasure and reward.

Bob soon adapted very well to his lowest-ranking position in the family pack, and all the human members of the family were pleased with the results of the corrective training.

Dogs who are possessive or jealous don't become this way overnight. Problems of this type are allowed to build up by the owners, who neglect to remind their dogs on a daily basis of their status—as dogs.

Barking

Barking is a dog's way of speaking. It sounds an alarm and warns other pack members of intruders, effectively warns off potential foes, and indicates a state of high excitement, such as during play.

While barking can be a positive reaction in appropriate situations—during play, or as a deterrent to intruders at home or would-be attackers while out walking—it can be negative when the dog barks inappropriately. Examples include barking every time someone walks by outside the house or continuing to bark at the door long after the dog has announced that a visitor has arrived.

TRAINER'S TIP

Some breeds are more vocal than others, so bear this in mind when choosing a dog—especially if you live in a residential area.

How do I deal with barking?

To deal with inappropriate barking, you must teach the dog that such noisy behavior is unrewarding and that quiet behavior is rewarding. Simply telling him to be quiet won't work because there is no incentive for him to obey. In fact, barking is rewarding to the dog because you are paying attention to him, so he will continue. In the dog's mind, any attention, even being told off, is better than none at all.

However, if you follow the command "quiet" with a reward when the dog responds, he'll quickly learn that "quiet" means a reward if he stops barking.

Achieving a conditioned response

When retraining, you have to be consistent and keep reinforcing what the dog has learned until the response is almost automatic. This is known as a conditioned response. Teaching a dog to do something without reinforcing the lessons doesn't work. To maintain a desired behavior, he needs "refreshers" every day.

Apply this to retraining a barking dog. Say that you've trained your dog to be quiet on command, but then on a couple of occasions, he barks when someone comes to the door and you don't correct him. The next time someone comes to the door, you do use the "quiet" command, but the dog ignores you. Now you have to go back several steps and start the training again.

Training him not to bark

1 When your dog barks for attention, ignore him until he settles down and is quiet. Avoid eye contact and fold your arms out of his reach.

2 When the dog realizes that you aren't responding to his barking, he will settle down to see what happens next. When he does, use the command "quiet" and reward him with a treat, praise, and attention. Once he has grasped the association between "quiet" and a reward, he'll start to obey. After this, praise and attention will be enough to maintain the response.

3 Another option is to take the dog out of the room when he barks inappropriately and let him back in only when he is quiet. When you let him in, use the command "quiet." If he barks, take him out again. He'll soon learn that barking is unrewarding (he is banished from the room) while being quiet is rewarding (he is allowed to rejoin his pack).

Noise nuisance

People often complain that their dogs bark in the house or yard when they are out all day. Why is this?

• The main reason is that left to his own devices, without companionship, the dog is quite simply bored and is looking for a way to amuse himself. Barking at passersby fulfills that need.

• Another reason is that the dog has taken on the responsibility of guarding the family home in your absence and is warning off potential intruders.

• The third reason, particularly if the dog howls rather than barks, is that he is calling to his pack to come home.

Depending on the reason for the behavior, you have various options for dealing with it.

• Have someone come in at least once during your absence to let the dog out and give him some exercise and attention. This will break up his day and reduce the time he has to wait for someone to come home.

• Supply your dog with a selection of activity toys to keep him occupied. These could include puzzle feeders filled with biscuits and a couple of stuffed Kongs, but be sure to deduct the amount of food that you give him in this way from his daily ration.

• Don't leave the dog in the yard, where he is more likely to react to passersby and other activity he can see. If for some reason, you don't want to leave him in the house, take him to a dog-sitter while you are out. This costs money, but the welfare of your dog is your responsibility, and you have a duty to your neighbors to see that your dog doesn't disturb them.

(continued)

4 You can also teach your dog to go to his bed or other designated area of the house and stay there quietly when he hears or sees something that would normally make him bark. Do this by telling him "bed" or "place," and give him some treats from a container when someone comes to the door or walks past the house. (Ask a friend to help you with this by ringing the doorbell, knocking on the door, or walking past the window.) The dog's focus will be on the treat rather than on barking.

5 Put the container next to the "quiet spot" so the dog can see it but not reach it. Reward him again if he is quiet and remains there. He will then regard this as a nice place to go to and be quiet, rather than bark. If you keep reinforcing this treat training, you should soon start to see improvement.

☑ Key points

- To prevent inappropriate barking, you must show the dog that an alternative behavior is more rewarding.

- If you're going to be out all day and you know your dog is likely to bark, take steps so that he isn't left alone to suffer separation anxiety or boredom. Employ a dog-sitter, take him to a kennel, and/or provide him with toys to keep him occupied.

- Enlist the help of a friend who can come to the door and knock or ring the bell so you can practice the training methods described.

- Use the training techniques whenever your dog barks inappropriately. Ignoring the training a few times may make your dog think it's fine to bark again, and you could find it more difficult to break the habit this time.

- Keep the training sessions short so your dog doesn't become bored or immune to the training, and always end on a positive note. If the dog responds instantly to a training method, end the session. Practice again the following day to reinforce what he's learned.

Using a spray collar

In cases where the dog is a habitual barker and all other suggested control options have failed, it's worth trying a spray collar. This collar is sound activated: When the dog barks, the collar emits a nonpainful but alarming spray of liquid (usually citronella-scented) under the dog's chin. He soon learns that not barking is much more rewarding: No barking, no sudden gush of smelly liquid under his chin.

There is also a remote control version of this collar, which lets you choose when to activate the spray, but you must do it the instant that inappropriate barking occurs, or the exercise will be pointless and confusing for the dog.

Case history: A confirmed barker

THE DOG • Toby, a three-year-old rottweiler.

THE PROBLEM • Toby barked from the window at passersby and at visitors to the house, and if he was put into another room, he would bark to be let out.

THE SOLUTION • Keith Davis paid Toby a home visit. The dog barked at the door and bounced around him as he entered. John, the owner, pulled Toby away, told him what a good boy he was, and shut him in another room. Keith deduced that Toby had assumed the role of pack leader in the house, with the responsibility for allowing visitors in and people to pass by outside. During the time Keith took to explain this to John, Toby stopped barking.

Keith went outside, then reentered the house. This time John ignored Toby, thereby removing any encouragement to continue barking. Keith also ignored the dog. Within a few minutes, Toby stopped jumping up and barking.

Next, Keith sat down and turned his body away from Toby as he conversed with John. Within a few minutes, Toby stopped barking; he paced back and forth between Keith and John, looking for guidance. After a few more minutes, he wandered off and lay down.

The next stage was to tell Toby what was expected of him. Keith stood up and moved around, but instead of letting the dog do what he thought he should do, John told him "quiet" and "stay." Toby did as he was told.

Keith advised John on how to break Toby's barking habit. The most important thing was to tell anyone who came to to the house to ignore Toby until he settled down.

A couple of weeks later, Keith went back to see how John was doing. When he entered the house, Toby barked a couple of times but didn't jump up. Then, not getting any response from either person, he quietly sat down. The dog's behavior at the window when people passed by had also improved and was continuing to do so.

Pulling on the leash

Curing a dog who pulls while you're walking him on the leash is quite simple when you know how. If the dog begins to move in front of you or starts to pull, stand still, put gentle tension on the leash, and wait for the dog to come back to your side. Then praise him, command him to "heel," and begin walking again.

As an experiment, try walking around the yard with your dog off the leash; use the "heel" command and your left hand to coax the dog to you. If this works, repeat the command, but this time put a treat in your left hand. Walk only 5 or 10 paces, then reward the dog.

Keep the treats in your left-hand pocket. Your dog will soon learn they are there, so he'll pay better attention to you and respond to your commands. Gradually increase the distance you walk between rewards.

You should find that this reinforcement of the "heel" command works quickly to stop your dog from pulling.

The element of surprise

1 If your dog pulls, don't pull back, since it will simply encourage him to strain harder at the leash. Instead, stop and walk backward. Surprised, the dog will stop and look to you for direction. Reposition him at your side with the command "heel" and resume walking. Repeat this exercise whenever necessary; the dog will soon realize that pulling is unrewarding and walking to heel is a much more relaxed experience.

2 Vary your pace while out walking: Jog, change direction, stop, and then walk on again. If your dog can't predict what you're going to do next, he will keep his attention on you rather than charging full steam ahead to what he thinks is his destination.

☑ Key points

- It's important to choose the right equipment, then fit and use it properly, so get advice from a trainer.

- Equipment alone won't cure a problem; you have to use training, too (see pages 58–61).

- Reinforce your position as pack leader at all times, in the house as well as outside. Dogs often pull if they think they're in charge.

- Don't let your dog stop and sniff the ground when walking, or he will soon train you to stop and start when he wants.

Using an antipull harness

1 If your dog is a strong puller, you may find an antipull harness helpful when you retrain him to walk at heel.

2 To fit the harness, gently place it over the dog's head.

3 Carefully draw his legs through the "armholes."

4 Check that the harness is not too tight and that no hair and/or folds of skin are uncomfortably trapped.

5 The harness will help you achieve more control, but don't jerk hard. If you hurt the dog, he may start pulling again in an effort to escape the discomfort. You must also check regularly to be sure the harness isn't chafing his legs or chest.

Case history: A quick fix

THE DOG • Blue, a two-year-old Labrador, was an extremely happy and energetic dog. He had been with his owner, Brenda, for 10 months.

THE PROBLEM • Blue was a big boy, and he pulled like a train when on the leash.

THE SOLUTION • Keith Davis found that Blue's flat leather collar was too small and his leash too short: Blue couldn't move more than 12 inches (30 cm) from Brenda's side without pulling.

Keith exchanged Blue's collar and leash for a headcollar, plus a Check-Choke collar and a leash of the right length, then took the dog for a walk. He used the pressure of just one finger and thumb on the leash and the gentle rattle of the chain to maintain the dog's attention. Then Brenda tried it, and, after learning how to use the new equipment, found she no longer had a problem. Brenda reported a week later that Blue was now a pleasure to take for walks.

Soiling in the house

Dog owners tend to get very annoyed when their pets soil in the house. This is understandable, but it's important to know why a dog does it. The most common reason is that he hasn't been housebroken correctly. The techniques for housebreaking puppies work for older dogs as well; see pages 46–47.

Persistence and timing

Some dogs dislike going out when the weather is cold or wet, preferring to relieve themselves in the comfort of their own home if they get the chance. If this is the case with your pet, be patient and, above all, persistent! Your dog will eventually get the idea that the sooner he goes, the sooner he will be back inside where it's warm and dry. Be sure to praise and reward him immediately so he views going outside as a positive and rewarding experience.

Pick the right times to take your dog out. If he's not ready to go, there is nothing you can do to hurry him. Get to know his habits by noticing how long it takes after he has eaten before he needs to relieve himself, because those are the obvious times to take him out. You may have to change your dog's feeding times so they fit your daily routine, or change your own schedule.

If your dog has an accident in the house, don't scold him. It will have no positive effect and will only confuse and frighten him. Simply clean up the mess, then clean the area thoroughly with a product designed to remove lingering odors that would attract your dog back to the same spot. Ordinary household cleaners aren't effective.

Take your dog outside shortly after he has eaten, since this is usually when he needs to relieve himself. At first, be prepared to wait a while for him to go, but when he does, praise and reward him lavishly. Try to encourage him to use the same spot each time so he associates that area with relieving himself. This will not only reinforce the behavior, it will also make cleaning up easier if you know where to look!

TRAINER'S **TIP**

If practical, put your dog's food and water bowls near where he has soiled inside so he won't want to return to the same spot. Generally, dogs don't eliminate near their eating, drinking, and sleeping areas.

☑ Key points

- Be prepared for housebreaking to take time. To lessen the damage to your house until your dog is trained, use see-through gates to restrict him to an area where it won't matter if he has an accident.

- Some dogs will let you know when they have to go out. They may be restless, whine, or stand by the door. Don't ignore these signals; take your dog outside right away.

- Never get cross with a dog for having an accident. The stress of having his owner angry with him may make his behavior worse.

- Arrange your dog's mealtimes to fit your schedule, or vice versa, so your pet has access to his designated bathroom area when required. Dogs usually need to go shortly after eating.

- You can train your dog to perform on command. To do this, use word association: As soon as your dog goes, say a word or phrase such as "go" or "hurry up" and then praise him. It won't be long before he learns that responding to the command earns him a reward.

Litter training

Some small breeds can be taught to use a litter box, which is practical if you don't have a yard or if you're away for long periods. Litter train in the same way that you would housebreak a puppy (see pages 46–47), with the litter tray taking the place of the outside location.

Choose a large, shallow tray (but not so shallow that the litter spills out) and line it with old newspaper or, preferably, a brand of cat litter that absorbs liquid and odor. Some pet stores also carry litter supplies made specifically for dogs.

Clean out the tray each time your dog uses it. Either double-bag the waste and put it in the trash, or bag it and place it in a special receptacle for dog waste if there's one nearby (use biodegradable plastic or paper bags).

When the tray gets too smelly or dirty, rinse it with warm water and a dash of nontoxic disinfectant, then dry it before refilling with clean paper or litter. It's important, however, not to disinfect over the dog's own odor too often, since this tells him where he should go.

Eating feces

A dog's habit of eating his own and other animals' excrement is revolting to us. However, because dogs' instincts tell them that eating droppings is perfectly natural and acceptable, it's important for owners to understand why they do it and not to get annoyed. Instead, discourage the habit by replacing it with a more desirable alternative.

Aversion therapy

First, you need to set the scene. This means collecting a selection of other animals' droppings to place in a specific training area. You also need a nontoxic, bitter-tasting solution designed for the purpose, which you can buy at a pet store or make yourself from mustard powder and water (see the Trainer's Tip on the opposite page).

For the training to have the best chance of working, you should consult your vet or a canine nutrition expert about the most suitable diet for your dog. If his food supplies all the nutrients he needs, he won't feel the need to eat droppings to satisfy a nutritional deficiency.

Making feces distasteful

1 Make the feces distasteful to the dog by spraying them liberally with an unpleasant-tasting liquid.

2 Walk your dog by the droppings, letting him investigate and taste them if he wants to. In most cases, he won't want to do it again.

☑ Key points

- Don't get angry with your dog for eating feces—it's only natural to him. Instead, learn how to change this habit into more acceptable behavior by teaching the dog to come to you for a reward instead of eating droppings.

- Be patient and persistent: This type of retraining can take some time and repetition.

- Make the effort to understand canine behavior (see pages 14–27), since this is the only way you can hope to relate to your dog effectively and achieve a better working partnership with him.

- Overcome your aversion to other species' idiosyncrasies; just because they are different doesn't mean they are abhorrent. If you can't cure them, learn to live with them, provided they're not harmful to anyone.

- Make sure your dog's diet contains all the nutrients he needs. Consult your vet or a qualified canine nutritionist on this point.

3 As the dog tastes the feces, interrupt him by calling him to you and using the "leave" command, rewarding him with a treat when he complies. The dog should now regard the droppings as unpleasant and turn his attention back to you, as this is more rewarding.

4 Practice walking by the droppings, saying "leave" and rewarding the dog when he obeys. He'll soon learn that leaving feces alone is more rewarding than eating them.

TRAINER'S TIP

Make feces distasteful by covering them with a foul-tasting solution, which most dogs won't touch, let alone eat. To make your own mustard solution, dissolve four heaping teaspoons of mustard powder in a little hot water and stir to make a smooth paste. Gradually add more warm water, stirring continuously, to make about 1 pint (0.5 liter). Let cool, then pour the solution through a funnel into an empty, well-washed liquid detergent bottle or other squeezable dispenser.

Nutritional needs

Why do dogs eat feces? We may as well ask why humans eat things that are usually totally abhorrent to a dog, such as pickled onions. It's often because the person feels the need for the nutrients that the particular food provides.

Animals utilize nutrients in food differently than humans do, and those that pass out in their droppings may be extremely desirable to or required by other animals whose bodies lack them. And, since animals don't necessarily view excrement the same way we do, some creatures are not repelled by ingesting their required nutrients in whatever form they present themselves, including feces.

Come back!

A dog who won't come back to his owner (recall) on command is a risk to himself and others. Don't let your dog off-leash without first doing some remedial work, or you'll simply reinforce the problem.

Loose dogs nearby, a bitch in season, children playing, or the smell of food are all common temptations that will make your dog disobey your recall command. You need to train him to follow your commands, rather than his instincts.

Teaching recall

1 If your dog's habit of not recalling is deeply ingrained, you need to find ways to overcome his indifference to you. Never go after your dog when he won't come back to you. He will think it's a great game if you chase him, so he'll find it rewarding.

☑ Key points

- Don't get angry with your dog when he won't come back to you; he's less likely to return if he knows he's going to be scolded.

- Don't blame the dog for not recalling; he can only respond as well as he has been taught.

- Don't feed your dog before a walk. If he's hungry, he's more likely to return to you for a food reward or want to go home for his meal.

- Don't call your dog back when you know he is unlikely to respond or you'll reinforce his behavior.

- Don't chase after your dog. Instead, walk, run away, or hide from him. He'll worry when he can't see you and may think he is being left, so he will run after you. When he reaches you, command him to sit and wait, then praise him. Don't always attach the leash when he returns.

- For initial recall training, see pages 76–79. Achieving good recall is something you really have to work at.

- Give your dog plenty of daily exercise and playtime. Dogs who don't get enough activity are more likely not to recall well.

2 If your dog won't return to you on command, walk or run away from him. He will think you're leaving him and come running, anxious not to be left behind. When he reaches you, stop and tell him to sit. Reward him with praise when he does, then walk on briskly; he's sure to follow. Repeat the exercise often, until your dog doesn't want to take his eyes off you in case you disappear.

3 Don't let your dog think that because you're holding the leash or reach for his collar, the walk is over, or he will be reluctant to recall. To avoid this, call the dog to you, tell him to sit, and reward him with a treat or toy. Next, play with his neck and collar, then give a release command such as "away" and send him off to play again. If you practice this often, your dog will learn that recall and leash don't always mean the end of playtime.

High-value rewards

Take your dog out for exercise when he's hungry, and wear a fanny pack or pouch containing tiny pieces of his favorite treats. Let him sniff the treats before you let him off the leash so he won't go far away. Recall and reward him with a treat; he'll soon realize that coming back to you on command is rewarding. Alternatively, use a high-value toy (see pages 72–75).

Make a game of recall by throwing your dog's favorite high-value toy for him to retrieve. You can make it more challenging by throwing the toy into long grass so he has to search for and scent it out. Making walks more exciting, so the dog's attention remains on you to see what you're going to do next, is the key to achieving and maintaining good recall.

Another way to deal with the problem is to recall your dog, reward him when he comes, attach the leash and walk for about 20 paces, then release him again. Practicing this every time you take your dog out for exercise will remove the "recall/leash/exercise over" association, making him more inclined to want to return to you.

When you do recall the dog, make sure your body language and tone of voice are encouraging and welcoming, or he won't be sure of a pleasant reception when he returns and may be inclined to stay away in case he's about to be scolded.

Hide and seek

This is a great way of motivating your dog to return to you. The game works on the principle of making the dog think you have disappeared and left him, so he will come to find you. The reward of seeking you out is then enhanced by a treat (initially) or a game with a high-value toy.

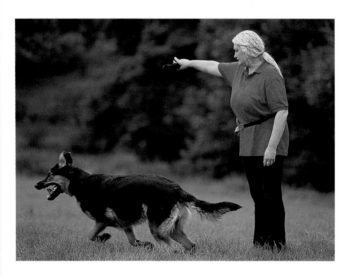

1 Send the dog away. This is reverse psychology, since the dog will think you don't want him and be more motivated to come back to you.

2 Once the dog is moving away from you, hide behind a tree or in bushes—but not too well at first. You don't want the dog to panic and run off in the opposite direction if he can't find you quickly.

3 If the dog appears to be struggling to find you, call him. When he does find you, call him to you, praise him lavishly, and give him a treat.

4 While he's distracted with the treat and relief at finding you, gently take hold of his collar and attach the leash. A word of warning, though: Don't always do this right away. Instead, play something else, repeat the hide-and-seek game, or walk on a little farther before the exercise session ends. Otherwise, your dog will associate the leash with the end of playtime and be reluctant to return to you.

Case history: Clicker solution

THE DOG • A five-year-old cross-breed named Trudy.

THE PROBLEM• Trudy and her owner, Liz, lived in a house that backed onto a field. When Trudy was let off the leash, she wouldn't come back; she also insisted on pulling Liz to the field. Once off-leash, she would race around, and if she saw other people she would run at them, barking.

THE SOLUTION • The first thing that trainer Keith Davis did was to check the equipment used for Trudy. Liz was using a short leash and a choke chain. The chain was tearing away the fur on Trudy's neck, so Keith suggested that Liz use a fabric collar and 8-foot (2.5-meter) training leash instead. Armed with some treats, a clicker, and an extra 20-foot (6-meter) leash, off they went to the field.

Keith decided that Trudy would be likely to respond to clicker training (see page 63), so he went through the concept of the exercise with Liz before putting it into practice. Trudy responded quickly; she really enjoyed the treats used to condition her to the "click," which she received each time her attention was focused on Liz. Then she was allowed a little more freedom, courtesy of the training leash; again, she responded well to the clicker. The instant she returned to Liz when called, Liz "clicked" and rewarded her, so Trudy associated coming back instantly on command with a pleasant experience.

Following Keith's instructions, Liz worked on these exercises every day. Two weeks later, Keith decided it was time to try the recall when Trudy was off-leash. A couple of training class members acted as distractions. Trudy was allowed to move away from Liz, but not to reach the "victims" before she was recalled. The distance between Trudy and Liz was gradually increased, to the point where Trudy went part of the way to the people and was then commanded to return. When she did, she was rewarded.

These exercises were followed up with regular recall reinforcement in training classes, and eventually Trudy could play with other dogs and recall on a single command.

Chasing

Dogs who chase after dogs, other animals, or even people are a liability and leave their owners open to possible prosecution. A dog may even end up losing his life if he bites someone or is caught bothering livestock. Having evolved as pack animals who must find, catch, and eat prey animals in order to survive, dogs have an instinct to chase anything that moves. Often, this is a playful practice pursuit, but in some instances, a dog will actually attack.

Get some help

It's important to get professional help with this problem, especially in the initial stages of training, since it's unlikely that you'll solve it on your own. Some dogs have a very strong inborn chase drive, and learning how to manage it requires firsthand practical help from an expert.

Disk training can be useful in retraining chasers, but you must learn how to do it correctly, or it will be worthless. Find a trainer who is experienced in using a disk. Gradual, controlled socializing may also prove useful, provided there is no risk or stress to the other people and animals involved.

The most important factors in retraining a chaser are to keep his attention firmly focused on you and to be sure that he understands and responds to "heel," "stay," and recall commands (see pages 58–61, 66–67, and 76–79). Also refer to pages 82–85 for ways to teach your dog his place within your family "pack."

☑ Key points

- If your dog reacts to dogs or other animals, find a good training school that offers socialization classes. Don't attempt to cure the problem on your own, since you're unlikely to succeed. Training classes are a must.

- It's important for initial socialization to occur in a controlled environment; if other dogs are involved, they should be nonreactive.

- Don't let a chaser off-leash in public places until retraining has been firmly established. Keep him on a long leash when retraining so you have control at all times. Don't release the dog from the leash too soon, or you could quickly undo weeks of work.

- Discover what motivates your dog to focus his attention on you: Is it a toy or a treat? Use your knowledge to the best advantage.

- Don't wait until the problem is beyond curing before you seek professional help. You will do neither yourself nor the dog any favors by waiting for him to grow out of it. The chances are he won't, and the problem will just get worse.

- Regular recall and socialization practice is essential in addition to what you do in training classes.

Distracting exercise

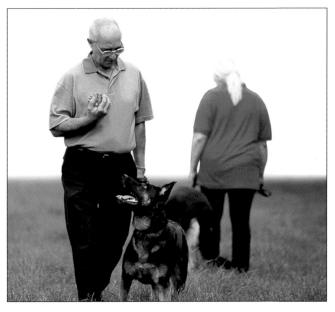

1 If a particular toy motivates your dog, use that as the distraction, or use a piece of his favorite treat. When approaching whatever it is that sparks the chase instinct, call the dog's name, command "heel" and "stay," and show him the toy or treat.

2 If the dog reacts to the "prey," simply ignore the behavior and call your dog's name, offering him the distraction. Reward him with it once you have passed the prey. Soon the dog will realize that staying with you is far more rewarding than chasing after another animal or a person.

TRAINER'S TIP

When practicing the distracting exercise, enlist the help of someone with a nonreactive dog. Using a retractable leash or a long line, gradually decrease the distance between your dog and your helper's dog until you are passing closely and your dog keeps his attention on you. Reward him for this.

Rivalry

Another potentially serious and certainly distressing problem for owners of two or more dogs is constant fighting. This is usually the result of an ongoing dispute over hierarchy, and it can be even more difficult to cure if the dogs are evenly matched in terms of sex, age, and size.

If the dogs are not neutered (or spayed, if the dogs are female), consult your vet about whether neutering one (usually the less dominant one) may help solve the problem. Sometimes it does, sometimes it doesn't.

Occasionally, if the rivalry is extremely intense, there is no alternative but to find a new home for one of the dogs.

Help to establish a hierarchy between two dogs by giving one privileges before the other. With your vet's advice, choose the apparently dominant dog. Give him attention first, feed him first, clip on his leash first before a walk, and so on. This way, the other dog will learn that he is farther down the pecking order and will not try to assert authority over his rival. In most cases, this will lead to a more harmonious relationship between the dogs; if it doesn't, you may want to consult a canine behaviorist to help you solve the problem. Ask your vet for a referral.

Case history: The importance of socialization

THE DOG • Samson was an 18-month-old Labrador who had been owned by Lorraine since he was 10 weeks old.

THE PROBLEM • Although good in all other respects, Samson would bark and leap around uncontrollably if he saw another dog, and Lorraine did not dare let him off the leash. She was seriously considering finding another home for him, but then a friend suggested that she take him to Keith Davis for training.

THE SOLUTION • In assessing Samson, Keith discovered that he had not been socialized with dogs and other animals properly, so he recommended socialization classes where Samson could meet other well-behaved and nonreactive dogs in a safe and controlled environment.

Having an expert at hand to show her what to do helped Lorraine deal with the situation more confidently and correctly than she could on her own. She realized that she had actually been making Samson's behavior worse by not allowing him to socialize with other dogs.

Once Samson was allowed to meet, greet, and play with other dogs, the problem resolved itself. He no longer saw them as potential foes and had no reason to react badly to them.

Climbing on furniture

If you don't want your dog on the furniture, set a precedent and don't let him on it in the first place. If he is a cute puppy or an adopted dog, you may feel that he deserves special privileges at first. After that, he will think it's his right to get on your furniture whenever he likes.

If you'd like the dog to sit on your lap or beside you, but only when you want him to, you have to set clear rules by teaching him that the only time he's allowed on the furniture is when you're there and you invite him to sit with you.

Training him to stay off the furniture

1 If your dog won't get off the furniture when you command him to, hook your finger into his collar to take control and say "off."

2 If the dog still won't move, gently but firmly remove him, repeating the command "off." If he tries to jump back on, sharply command "no." If he tries again, again say no and put him out of the room. Let him back in a short time later and tell him to lie down; if he tries to get back on the furniture, put him out of the room again. He'll learn that getting on the furniture is unrewarding (he's banished from the room), while if he stays down, he's allowed to remain with you.

3 To keep your dog off furniture when you can't monitor him, put obstacles in the way to prevent him from jumping up.

TRAINER'S TIP

With a persistent offender or when retraining, use a see-through gate. This way, he can still see what's going on and won't feel isolated, but he won't have access to the furniture.

✓ Key points

• When you first acquire your dog, decide what the rules about his being on the furniture will be. You may regret ever allowing him on the sofa when the novelty has worn off and the upholstery is covered with dog hair.

• If the dog is never to be allowed on the furniture, all members of the household must enforce the rule, or the dog will be confused.

• If you're going to be away, stop the dog from jumping on furniture by restricting his access to it with a see-through gate, closed door(s), or obstacles.

• If the dog approaches a sofa or chair with the intent of jumping up, command "no" and be sure he obeys.

Case history: Furniture fanatic

THE DOG • Bess was a large, two-year-old cross-breed German shepherd. Paul had owned her since she was nine months old, and in the first few weeks of living with him, she had been ill. Succumbing to her soulful eyes, Paul had allowed her to sleep in his bedroom until she recovered.

THE PROBLEM • Paul didn't realize what a problem he was allowing to develop. It wasn't long before Bess began to climb onto the bed during the night. Eventually she claimed the sofa downstairs as well, and no one could sit on it if Bess was *in situ*.

THE SOLUTION • Trainer Keith Davis was called in to help. After assessing the situation, he concluded that Bess had taken control of the household and was taking as much advantage of this as possible. He advised Paul to ignore her when she came to him for attention, thereby relegating her to second place and reinstating himself as the pack leader. She was also banned from the bedroom.

Keith also suggested introducing Bess to an indoor crate (see pages 44–45) as a place she could call her own and in which she could feel secure. This was done, and she accepted the crate almost immediately. When she was put in it the first night, she objected at first but soon discovered that whining for attention brought no results. A couple of nights later, Bess had settled into her new routine without further fuss.

At this point, the crate door was left open overnight. Paul placed small items of furniture on the sofa and chairs so that Bess couldn't climb onto them. This strategy also worked.

The next step was to remove the crate but keep the obstacles on the furniture overnight to reduce Bess's habit of climbing on it. Gradually, over a few weeks, she became less and less inclined to seek out furniture on which to lie, and Paul stopped restricting her access to it. She didn't return to her old habits.

Begging and fussy eating

Dogs who beg at the table or are fussy eaters generally have one thing in common—they have been allowed to get away with this behavior.

The two also tend to go hand in hand because dogs who are given human food seem to prefer it above all else. This is because dogs are instinctively scavengers and because they want to eat what their human pack leaders eat.

In rare cases, fussy eating can indicate an underlying medical problem, so if your dog has recently started to turn his nose up at whatever you feed him and displays symptoms such as digestive disturbances, skin ailments, rapid weight loss, and poor coat condition, take him to the vet for an examination to make sure he isn't allergic to the food he's being given.

Dog food, whether wet, semi-moist, or dry, can go bad, which can make it unappetizing for your dog, so always follow the storage instructions on the can or package. Avoid buying a large bag of food unless you're able to use it quickly once it has been opened, or transfer it into airtight containers. Finally, always check the sell-by date on the package.

Begging

To deter begging at the table, there are several steps you can take.

• Remove the dog from the room while you are preparing food and eating.

• If your dog responds to being sent away to lie down and stay, do this every time the family sits down to eat. Make sure everyone in the household is aware of and abides by the rule of not giving the dog human food tidbits, since this will encourage him to beg.

• Steel yourself not to give in to your dog's pleading expression and soulful eyes. Insist that he go away from the table and not come harassing you for food.

If your dog fully understands his place at the bottom of your family pack, and doesn't need this to be reinforced (see page 85) try feeding him at the same time you have your own meal so he has something to distract him. It's a good idea to insist that he lie down quietly after eating while you finish your meal.

Training him to eat what he's given

1 Measure out your dog's ration for the morning, then split it in half. Do the same with the evening meal if he is fed twice a day.

2 Put down half of the food for the dog.

3 If he eats it within a few minutes, put down the other half.

4 After 20 minutes, remove any uneaten food and throw it away. Don't give the dog any other food, including treats, until his next mealtime. Be sure that he has a constant supply of fresh, clean water.

Curing a fussy eater

Once your vet has established that your dog is not ill and the food you are providing is suitable for his needs, follow the method above, and he'll be eating up his food within a week. He will learn that the food he is given is all he is going to get, and since dogs won't allow themselves to go hungry, the problem will be solved!

☑ Key points

- Don't hand-feed your dog tidbits in an effort to get him to eat. It's not necessary and will simply make him even fussier.

- Be sure that no one else in the family gives him tidbits, either from the table or between meals.

- Don't keep changing your dog's food in an effort to encourage him to eat. Provided your vet says it's suitable, keep him on the same diet.

- Never leave uneaten food so the dog can help himself whenever he feels like it. Be strict: Remove the food if he doesn't eat it at mealtimes so he learns that he either eats when you let him or goes hungry until the next mealtime.

- Vary the times of day that you feed your dog so he never knows when he will next be fed. This will give him an incentive to eat the food you give him when it is given.

Chewing

Dogs who chew things they shouldn't can soon wreck a house, so it's essential to put a stop to this destructive behavior swiftly. Dogs chew for a number of reasons:

- To help them teethe (in the case of young dogs)
- Because they are bored
- Because it gives them pleasure

In all cases, the result for the dog is rewarding, so you must provide him with an alternative that is just as rewarding for him and more acceptable to you, while reinforcing the lesson that the dog can chew only certain items that you provide for that purpose.

Restricted access

During retraining, when you are unable to keep an eye on your dog (such as when you are out or are busy elsewhere in the house), restrict him to an area in which he cannot do much, if any, damage (and certainly where there are no accessible electrical wires). Provide him with a chew toy that he can demolish or an activity toy such as a filled Kong (see page 31) to keep him occupied. If there is no suitable area in the house, use a crate (see pages 44–45).

☑ Key points

- Never encourage your dog to pull or chew at clothing during play sessions. This can lead to inappropriate chewing and aggressive, dominant behavior, including biting.

- Don't give the dog items of old clothing or discarded shoes to play with, or he will view all clothing or shoes, unwanted or not, as fair game.

- Never allow your dog to chew sticks or lumps of wood, since he may not differentiate between them and your table legs. In addition, wood splinters can cause serious injury, and dogs have become impaled on sticks.

- A bored dog will find his own entertainment, so always provide him with suitable playthings.

- Spray items that your dog persists in chewing with a nontoxic, bitter-tasting anti-chew liquid, available at pet stores.

Teaching him that chewing is unrewarding

1 Have some shake cans—lidded containers half-filled with pebbles—accessible around the house to use when you see your dog chewing inappropriately.

2 Throw a shake can so it lands near the dog (obviously, don't aim to hit him!) to interrupt the chewing. As it lands, the dog will stop chewing or jump away in surprise. If you don't feel confident about your aim or if you have a very nervous dog, simply rattle the can hard instead.

3 Quickly replace the item that he was chewing with a toy or chew treat that he can nibble on instead. Encourage him to take it and chew it.

4 Give the dog an activity toy filled with something tasty to keep him occupied, especially if you are busy, so he doesn't get bored and go looking for something inappropriate to chew for entertainment.

5 If your dog enjoys chewing particular items, such as shoes, table legs, or soft furnishings, buy a nontoxic anti-chew spray (available at pet stores) and treat those items. Then encourage your dog to have a nibble. He'll find this most unrewarding because of the nasty taste and won't be likely to try it again.

TRAINER'S TIP

It's a twofold problem when your dog grabs the mail as the mailman is putting it through the slot and then rips it to shreds. To solve this quickly and easily, either put a separate mailbox outside your front door or attach a wire drop box to the door over the slot so the mail is protected when it drops through.

Door manners

A dog who pushes past his owner and rushes to the door when company comes is a real nuisance. Not only could this result in an accident if you trip over him, but people may become reluctant to visit if they know they're going to be jumped on when they enter the house. Few people like an ill-mannered dog. To prevent this behavior, try any of the strategies on the following pages.

Use the reward container technique (see pages 68–69) whenever someone comes to the door. Your dog will soon learn that going to his designated place and staying there when visitors knock is more rewarding than rushing to the door to greet them. Remember to reward your dog for correct behavior. Eventually this becomes a conditioned response, and you'll need to use treats only occasionally; verbal praise will be sufficient the rest of the time.

If your house layout allows it, put a see-through gate across the hall to deny your dog access to the door. Once your visitors are inside, they should ignore the dog until he settles down, then say hello to him.

Teaching him good door manners

1 First, enlist another person to help you practice this exercise. Also, review sit and stay training (see pages 62–63 and 66–67). When a visitor comes to the door, command your dog to sit and stay before you open it.

2 Greet your visitor and tell her to ignore the dog until you decide to call him over to say hello. Don't wait too long at first, because if the dog's excitement gets the better of him and he ignores your "stay" command, it may set the training back a step. If the dog does approach without your permission, tell your visitor to ignore him until he has settled down and you can reinstate the sit-stay position.

3 Repeat the "sit-stay" command, then let your visitor greet the dog, but instruct her to ignore him if he rushes over or jumps up. Once the dog has been greeted, you can either let him stay with you and the visitor or send him to lie down quietly. Constant reinforcement of this exercise will soon teach the dog that rushing to the door is unrewarding, while not doing so results in pleasant interaction with guests.

✓ Key points

- If you are unable to control your dog at the door, ensure his safety and that of your visitors by putting him in another room.

- Remember that *you* are the pack leader in your home, not your dog, so don't let him greet visitors before you do.

- Command your dog to sit and stay before attaching the leash to take him for a walk.

- Never allow your dog to push through a door before you. Make him wait, even if it takes several minutes to reinforce by using the door-shutting exercise (see pages 122–123). Add the command "wait" to the exercise as your dog does so, and reward him when he complies.

- Continual, consistent command reinforcement is the only way to teach your dog what you require of him.

Pushing through doors

Does this look familiar? Curing this habit is quite simple when you know how. You'll need someone to act as a visitor, then you can implement the retraining procedure.

Teaching him to wait

1 Put the dog on the leash and stand by the door, waiting for your helper to knock or ring. When he does, open the door a little way.

2 At this point, the dog will try to barge through to see who's there.

3 When he does, slam the door shut (being careful not to trap his nose); the dog will jump back in surprise.

4 Practice this a few times, until the dog doesn't try to push past you when someone knocks and you open the door, but instead stands quietly, watching and waiting to see what you're going to do next. He has discovered that pushing past you is unpleasant because the door is shut in his face.

5 Next, command your dog to sit and stay as you open the door. When he does, reward him. He'll learn that waiting while you answer the door is more pleasant than trying to push through it. Gradually, you can work toward opening the door wider each time. The next step is to teach your dog to remain in the sit-stay while guests enter, as explained on pages 120–121.

Travel problems

Dogs who are reactive in the car—barking, jumping about, and soiling or vomiting—are generally this way because the sight of the world going by upsets them and the vehicle's motion makes them feel queasy.

In addition, if you only ever travel with your dog to the vet's office for treatment, he will associate the vehicle with something unpleasant and will be unsettled while in transit.

Car safety

Don't let your dog jump out of the car until you are sure it's safe, both for him and for others. If your dog insists on barging his way out regardless, you need to retrain him.

Some dogs respond well to a travel harness. Make sure it fits comfortably and correctly—snugly enough that he can't escape, but not so tightly that it causes discomfort.

☑ Key points

- Never let your dog travel unsecured in a vehicle. It's not safe for either the dog or the driver and passengers.

- Don't let your dog jump out of the car before you are ready for him to get out.

- If you are traveling with your dog in a crate, cover it so he can't see anything at which to bark.

- When getting the dog in and out of the car, vary your timing: Let him jump in or out only when you are ready.

- Attaching a long leash to the dog's collar or headcollar and tugging on it, while simultaneously saying "no," may help stop reactive behavior in the car.

- Putting a headcollar on a dog when transporting him can help to improve his behavior by giving him something to think about other than reacting to anything he sees.

- When your dog is in transit, drive smoothly. Get him used to traveling by taking only short trips at first.

Put a reactive dog in a travel crate (some indoor crates can also be used in vehicles) to transport him. (See pages 44–45 for how to crate train your dog.) Put the dog's blanket in with him for familiarity, along with his favorite toy and an activity toy to keep him occupied and distracted. Cover the crate with a sheet or blanket; if the dog can't see out, he won't see anything to which he could react. Covering the crate has a calming effect and is well worth trying.

1 When you start to open the door, the dog will come close to it with his head down, ready to leap out.

2 As he does, close the door, and the dog will leap back in surprise. Keep repeating this exercise until he stays away from the door as you open it.

3 Attach the leash securely, tell the dog to sit or stay, and reward him.

4 Once you are satisfied that it's safe, let the dog out and tell him to come to heel and sit so you can close the door and lock the car. Practice this every time you take him out of the car.

Case history: Terrier travel

THE DOG • Missy was a small terrier type, 18 months old. Her owner, Doreen, had brought her home from an animal shelter three weeks earlier.

THE PROBLEM • When traveling in the car, Missy barked at anything and everything she saw. She was free to sit where she wanted, and she ended up jumping from seat to seat in order to get a better vantage point from which to bark. She could—and did—"chase" a dog, passerby, or cyclist through 360 degrees around the inside of the car! Doreen could not cope with Missy's behavior any longer: It was "cure or go back" time.

THE SOLUTION • Keith Davis explained to Doreen that the best way to deal with a problem of this type is to secure the dog in the car in a travel harness or crate placed in the rear of a station wagon or SUV or on the back seat of a sedan. Doreen had a crate, so Keith showed her how to position it in the car. He then advised her to give Missy an activity toy to keep her occupied and to cover the crate with a blanket. He explained that if the dog couldn't see anything to bark at, she would stay quiet.

Keith's advice worked: Doreen still has Missy, who now travels contentedly and quietly in the covered crate.

RESOURCES

IN THE UNITED STATES

Breeder/Breed Information

American Kennel Club
(headquarters)
260 Madison Ave.
New York, NY 10016
Phone: (212) 696-8200
Website: www.akc.org
*Breed information, breeder referrals,
and advice on choosing a dog.*

Kennel-Search
Website: www.kennel-search.com
*Links to breeders, trainers, groomers,
rescue groups, and equipment suppliers.*

Puppy Dog Web
Website: www.puppydogweb.com
*Breeders' directory, breed profiles, ads
for purebred dogs, and links to rescue
and breed organizations.*

Equipment

Coastal Pet
Website: www.coastalpet.com
Check-Choke collars, training supplies.

Doctors Foster & Smith
P.O. Box 100
Rhinelander, WI 54501-0100
Phone: 1-800-381-7179
Website: www.drsfostersmith.com
*Training supplies, toys, food, parasite
control products, and prescription
medications; free catalog.*

The Leash Connection
303 County Road 44
Clayton, AL 36016
Phone: (334) 775-3647
Website: http://dog-training.com
E-mail: info@dog-training.com
*Wholesale training supplies and videos,
grooming products, food, and toys.*

The Pet Street Mall
Website: www.petstreetmall.com
Phone: 1-800-957-5753
*Dog beds, crates, doghouses, and other
supplies; pet helpline.*

Training

American Dog Trainers Network
Website: www.inch.com/~dogs
Helpline: (212) 727-7257 (1:00–3:00
p.m. EST, 7 days)
E-mail: dogs@inch.com
*Resources for training, behavior
problems, and many other topics.*

The Association of Pet Dog Trainers
17000 Commerce Parkway, Suite C
Mt. Laurel, NJ 08054
Phone: 1-800-PET-DOGS (738-3647)
Website: www.apdt.com
*Directory of recommended books and
videos; links to trainers.*

IN CANADA

Breeder/Breed Information

The Canadian Kennel Club
(headquarters)
89 Skyway Ave. Suite 100
Etobicoke, ON M9W 6R4
Phone: 1-800-250-8040 or (416) 675-
5511
Client services: (416) 674-3699
Website: www.ckc.com
*Membership in the Canadian Kennel
Club includes a subscription to* Dogs in
Canada, *a monthly magazine. Website
showcases nearly 200 dog breeds with a
photo and description of each breed.
Provides an extensive listing of breeders
across Canada. Website at: www.dogs-
in-canada.com*
E-mail: information@ckc.ca

Equipment

Mayer's Online Pet Shop
3038 Danforth Ave.
Toronto, ON M4C 1N2
Phone: (416) 694-5342
Website: www.mayerspet.net
E-mail: info@mayerspet.com

Nature Pet Centres
Complexe Pointe-Claire
6321 Trans-Canada Highway
Pointe-Claire, QC H9R 5A5
Phone: (514) 694-3291
Website: www.naturepet.com
E-mail: info@naturepet.com

Petcetera
1565 Cliveden Ave.
Delta, BC V3M 6P7
Phone: (604) 526-4180
Website: www.petcetera.ca

Training

Canadian Association of Professional
Pet Dog Trainers
Jan Morgan, Administrative Assistant
P.O. Box 59011
Whitby, ON L1N 3V6
Phone: 1-877-SIT-STAY (748-7829)
Website: www.cappdt.ca
E-mail: pawsitivepuppies@sprint.ca

INDEX

ACKNOWLEDGMENTS

Executive Editor Trevor Davies
Executive Art Editor Leigh Jones
Editor Katy Denny
Designer Jo Tapper
Picture Researcher Jennifer Veall
Production Controller Ian Paton
Photographer Angus Murray
Indexer Indexing Specialists (UK) Ltd